FETCH

EVERY JACK MUST HAVE HIS JILL

M VIOLET

Cover Design by COFFIN PRINT DESIGNS. All stock photos licensed appropriately.
Edited by Kat Wyeth (Kat's Literary Services)
Formatted by Champagne Book Design

For information on subsidiary rights, please contact the publisher at authormviolet@gmail.com

A NOTE FROM THE AUTHOR

FETCH is a dark MF stalker romance novella set in the world of on-line gaming and loosely inspired by the Jack and Jill nursery rhyme. This book is intended for adults 18 years and older ONLY. If you are not over the age of 18, please put this book down and back away.

This is a dark romance with many sensitive subjects and scenes that may not be suitable for everyone. Please refer to my extensive list of CWs on my website.

If you've made it this far, get ready for a quick and dirty ride inside the minds of two of the most fucked-up characters I've ever written.

For all my dark romance,
gamer-girlies who have ever
simped over a faceless voice.

FETCH PLAYLIST

Take It From The Top—The Velveteers

You're So Pretty—mehro

Wet Girl—Kazaku

PRAY TO ME—DeathbyRomy & Palaye Royale

take me down—hazel

Rebel Yell—Billy Idol

Worship—Magnolia Park, PLVTINUM & Vana

Button Eyes—The Pretty Wild

PLEASER—Vana

GUNGHO—VUKOVI

Heart-Shaped Box—Nirvana

Damned—The Holy Knives

BREADCRUMBS—YAS

SMUT—Jutes

Heart-Shaped Box—Annaca

Mr. Sandman—SYML

WORTHY—KNIFE BRIDE

Damage—The Haunt

Superglue—Neoni

Sex Machina—bludnymph

Don't You (Forget About Me)—Simple Minds

Taste of the Divine—Shaker, Azee & Cobra

Jack and Jill went up the hill
To fetch a pail of water.
Jack fell down and broke his crown,
And Jill came tumbling after.
Then up got Jack and said to Jill,
As in his arms he took her,
"Brush off that dirt for you're not hurt,
Let's fetch that pail of water."

—"Jack and Jill", Nursery Rhyme.

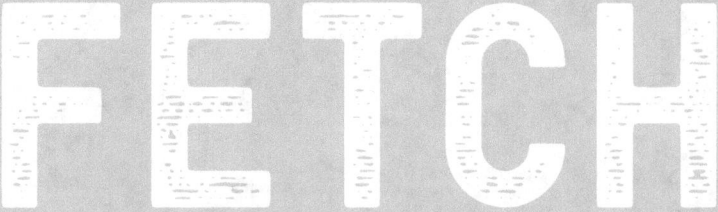

PROLOGUE

ROXY

THE LINE TO GET INTO JOYSTICK TONIGHT is already wrapped around the block. I walk past it and hand the bouncer my VIP ticket. A cackle of boos rings out behind me. I turn to them and shrug. "Perks of being a sponsor, boys."

Technically, *I'm* not a sponsor. My work is. The pay might be shitty at Vinyl Delights, but nights like these make up for it. Our little record store is one of many local businesses collaborating to bring Lavender Heights the biggest gaming event it's ever seen.

As a diehard gamer girl myself, I wouldn't miss this for anything. Plus, Juniper would kill me if I made her come alone with only Coast and Milo to hang out with. We tolerate them at work, but neither of us wants to hang out with them all fucking night.

They're good looking and polite enough, but their taste in music is weird. And they're semi-obsessed with Juniper. When we all work together, they just gawk at her and let her pick the music in the store. I think it's kind of cute but it gives Juniper the ick.

My gorgeous friend waves to me from the bar, her blonde hair reflecting tones of pink from the glare of the neon lights. "Damn, lady, you look spicy. These gamer boys are going to think you're one of the snacks."

I feel my cheeks blush. Juniper is an exhibitionist, and I usually hide my curves behind hoodies and jeans. But tonight, I want to *look* like a VIP. I twirl around, showing off my short organza skirt. It's black with sparkles.

"I'm flaunting tonight," I say as I lean forward and squeeze my arms together, showing off my deep cleavage. The ribbons on my black bustier are hot pink, matching the lights overhead. I paired the entire ensemble with high-top wedged sneakers. You never know when you're gonna have to run away. Heels are a death trap. I hate them. Especially after my accident.

She fingers a lock of my dark-brown hair. "I love the waves too."

"*You* always look hot," I praise. Juniper leans against the bar in a tight white bodysuit, rhinestone stiletto heels, and a brown, faux-fur jacket.

She puckers her bright-pink lips around the straw of her pink drink and winks. "Thanks, babe. Coast and Milo already came by to tell me that very same thing."

I burst out laughing. "They did not. Those two would have a heart attack before that happens."

She winks again. "I know, but it's what they're thinking. Fucking weirdos."

I glance around the bar, taking in the sights. They did an amazing job transforming our local arcade bar into a gamer's wet dream. In between each vintage arcade machine is a server dressed up as an iconic game character, holding a tray of brightly colored shots. Cassette tapes and vinyl records strung together act as garland in between the aisles. And in the center of the room is an old-school photo booth. A pair of drunk girls stumble out wearing pink boas and star-shaped sunglasses. *There's so much glitter everywhere.*

The speakers are pumping out old-school, classic eighties music. I bob my head to "Don't You (Forget About Me)" by Simple Minds. while Juniper and I peruse the hors d'oeuvres table. Keeping with the eighties theme, there are mini sloppy-joes sandwiches, a cheese fondue station, deviled eggs, and Popsicles for dessert. There are also trays of lollipops, Jell-O shots, and candy cigarettes.

I grab a shot while Juniper settles for a Popsicle to satisfy her oral fixation. "So, you think Punk will make an appearance?"

My stomach flips. "*Punk Wilder?* He's an enigma. I highly doubt it," I answer while trying to keep the disappointment out of my voice.

Punk Wilder is one of the most famous skaters of our generation. Tonight's party is to celebrate the five-year anniversary of his skateboarding game. But what makes him more intriguing is the fact that he hasn't been seen in public since its launch. And who could blame him?

Juniper twirls her tongue around the tip of the Popsicle like it's something tastier. "Yeah, after *that* scandal, I wouldn't show my face in public either."

"Shit happens. I think everyone deserves a second chance." I feel bad for the guy. After his injury, he spiraled. *I can definitely relate to that.*

She shrugs. "Well, at least he didn't lose *all* his sponsors. Otherwise, this dope party would not be happening."

I don't play extreme sports games, preferring the first-person shooter ones instead. But I respect the impact his franchise has had on our community. Every little skater boy and girl plays that game like it's a rite of passage. Which is why Joystick also set up a skate ramp in the back parking lot as well.

"Oh fuck. *Incoming*," Juniper says under her breath. She rolls her eyes and turns her back toward the crowd.

I can't help but chuckle as Coast and Milo make their way toward us. They barely look at me. "Quit pretending you don't love that they're obsessed with you."

She winces as if I slapped her. "Lies. They are so fucking cringe."

"Hey, Juniper," Milo rasps. At five foot ten, he just barely bests her in height. Especially in those four-inch heels she's wearing. Coast, on the other hand, towers over her.

She lets out a dramatic sigh for emphasis as she spins around. "What's up?"

"Cool party," Coast quips. His long black eyelashes are to die for. They frame his big brown eyes like spider webs.

Juniper shrugs.

"We are having a great time," I answer for her as I try to conceal a giggle.

"Okay, bye, see you at work tomorrow." Juniper grabs me by the wrist and drags me to the other side of the bar. "Ugh, they are so awkward."

"I think it's sweet. You just don't like nice guys," I semi-tease.

Juniper has a new toxic boyfriend every other week. My dating life, on the other hand, is nonexistent. Ever since my injury, I haven't felt like myself. Other than an occasional random hookup, I don't have the desire to get close to anyone.

Spending three years with a man who I thought was *the one*, only to have him treat me like damaged goods after I lost my dance scholarship… it sent me to a dark place. Even though my leg has healed, my heart hasn't.

"You want another drink?" she yells over the music.

I nod. "Snag me a couple more Jell-O shots. I'm going to hit the ladies' room."

I push my way through the ever-growing crowd. I'm not used to seeing Joystick so busy. It takes me ten minutes to get to the stairwell that leads down to the bathrooms. I praise myself internally for opting for the sneaker wedges instead of high heels as I make my descent. The floors are slippery and sticky with splashes of booze and broken pieces of candy.

I groan when I see the line heading into the women's restroom. There are at least fifteen girls ahead of me in the darkened hallway. "Fuck this," I mutter under my breath.

I charge past them and head for the exit, remembering the gas station next door. I shiver as I jog across the parking lot through the cold rain. I'll have to show my ticket again at the door, but there's no way I can drink anymore if I don't pee.

I get the key from the attendant and go as fast as I can. I wash my hands twice before returning the key and heading back to Joystick. I make it as far as the side of the building, near an exit door that apparently doesn't allow reentry. I start to knock on it when a hand clamps down on my wrist.

What the fuck? I spin around to face the culprit.

"Hey, sexy. Where you running off to?" A tall beefy dude with reddish-brown hair leers down at me.

I snatch my wrist away. "I'm just trying to get back inside."

He smirks. "Nah, I think you're looking for some company. Stay and show me what you got underneath that skirt."

My stomach knots as I glance down the alleyway. There are

loads of people just around the corner, but over here, we're isolated. And the music is too loud for anyone to hear me if I scream.

I back up toward the locked exit door. "I'm good, actually. My friends are just inside. Wanna meet them?" Maybe if I can get him to follow me inside, I'll have a better shot at shaking him.

He inches forward, forcing me against the concrete wall. "I like it better out here." Before I can react, he clamps a hand over my mouth. I let out a muffled scream and try to kick forward, but he has me pinned.

"Shhh. I'll be quick." He stuffs his free hand underneath my skirt and yanks my panties to the side.

Oh no. Fuck. I can't breathe. This can't be happening. I lift my leg and knee him in the groin as hard as I can. His grip on my mouth slips, and I bite his hand before pushing him back. I spin around to make a run for it when he grabs a hold of my hair.

"Come back here, bitch!" He pins me against the exit door.

Tears stream down my cheeks. No. "Please, let me go."

His eyes darken as he reaches under my skirt again. This time, I freeze. Bile rises in my throat as he slips a chubby finger inside my panties. "That's better. Hold still while I touch you."

My heart races, beating up into my throat. I look away as he rubs his finger against my slit. He tugs on my waist with his free hand, coaxing me forward. "Come on, my truck's just right over there."

Fuck. I shove at him. "No. I need to get back inside."

He growls and pushes me back against the wall. "Fine. We'll do it here." He shoves his finger inside me, and I almost black out. "You're pretty tight for a whore."

The door barrels open beside us, and he jumps back, releasing me. "Hey!" The sound of techno music and shrill voices echoes into the lonely alleyway.

I don't hesitate and make a run for it, pushing past the bathroom line. I sprint up the stairs and don't stop until I spot Juniper.

I crash into her, collapsing against her. "He-he tried to…"

"Roxy, what's wrong? Did someone hurt you?" Juniper cups my face in her hands, her eyes searching for any signs of injuries.

I shake my head as the tears pour out. "No-no. I mean, yes. He touched me…"

Juniper looks around. "Is he still here? I will fucking cut his dick off."

"It was outside. I went next door to use the bathroom. I'm sorry," I cry.

"You have nothing to be sorry for." She whips out her phone. "I'm calling the cops, and then I'm going to help you sue the fuck out of this place."

I grab her hands. "No. Please. No cops. I just want to go home."

She arches an eyebrow at me. "Roxy, you were assaulted. That guy is still out there. We have to tell someone."

Fuck. I don't want any more attention on me. I can't take another scandal. "Fine. You can call them after we leave. Tell them you saw it but that you don't know who it was."

She nods. "Where did he touch you?"

I shake my head again. "Doesn't matter. The back door opened, and I ran inside as fast as I could."

"Everything okay?" Coast interrupts from seemingly out of nowhere. "You both look upset."

Juniper rolls her eyes and drapes an arm around me. "We're fine. She's just got food poisoning. Stay away from the sloppy joes, boys."

"Thank you," I whisper as we leave Milo and Coast standing there dumbfounded.

It took me twenty minutes to convince Juniper that I was fine being alone in my apartment. After I showed her my pistol, she conceded. This is Lavender Heights. Every single woman living alone should have one.

As I stand under the piping hot water of my shower, scrubbing my skin raw with a loofa filled with peach bodywash, I become angrier. *I'm angry with myself.* I know better than to wander around in the dark alone on a Friday night in that part of town.

What the fuck was I thinking?

I'm just grateful to whoever used that back door to leave. They don't even know how close I was to… Fuck. I pinch my eyes shut and try and block it out. I'm fine. I'm okay. I'm safe now. Remembering the exercises my therapist taught me, I exhale a deep breath and count to ten. Another deep breath in through my nose. And out. And repeat.

The muscles between my shoulder blades begin to loosen the longer I do this. Satisfied that I've managed to stave off another full-blown panic attack, I turn off the water and step out to dry off.

I slip into a pair of fuzzy sweats, pour a glass of whiskey, and melt into my couch. I'm tired but still on edge. I know I won't be able to sleep, so why bother? I click on the TV and channel surf until I stumble on an old rom-com. Within minutes, I relax even more. Until my phone pings three times in a row.

I look down to see a string of texts from Juniper.

Have you seen this? What the fuck is going on at Joystick tonight? Girl, this is all over the fucking news.

My fingers tremble, hovering over the link she sent me. I try to swallow, but my mouth is dry. My nerves are shot. I don't know how much more I can take right now.

She texts again.

Roxy??? Is this the guy?

Fuck. I click on the link, and all the blood rushes to my feet. Thank fuck I'm sitting down. The first line reads: *Man jumps to his death at popular arcade bar, Joystick, tonight. Leaves behind a note confessing to sexual assault.*

I sit forward, my heart racing. What the fuck? There's no way. That creep didn't strike me as the remorseful type.

I text her back.

I don't know. They haven't released his photo yet.

Typing bubbles appear, disappear, then reappear again.

It has to be. Shit. Are you okay?

I don't know what to feel. Or think. I take a sip of my whiskey and read through the article again. The reporter states that no onlookers recalled seeing the man inside. And the bar had zero record of him being on the guest list. It must be him. He must have weaseled his way inside after I ran through the back door.

But for what purpose? I find it hard to believe he killed himself just moments after I got away from him. A shiver snakes up my back. It just doesn't add up. And I hate that I'm a part of it.

I text her back.

No one can ever know what happened to me tonight. Okay? No one.

Juniper has been my best friend since I left school three years ago. I trust her with my life. But I need to make sure she keeps quiet.

I understand. We left before it happened, so I doubt anyone will contact us. But I'm deleting all these texts just in case.

I let out a sigh of relief and delete the texts on my end as well. I just want to put this night behind me and forget I ever went to Punk Wilder's anniversary party. The one he didn't even bother to show up to. Ugh.

I down the rest of my whiskey and switch my TV over to my gaming console. I need to shoot some apocalyptic creatures to blow off steam. When I load into *After: 8113*, I see that Juniper has the same idea. Her gamer tag, BratBaby, pops up on my screen. I accept her group party invite and turn on my headphones.

"There she is. Ready to fuck some shit up, JillChick22?" Juniper asks.

I unmute my mic. "Fuck, yes, I am."

This is the only place where I'm in control. I can do anything in this game. *I can be anyone.* And tonight, I need to be someone other than the girl who got sexually assaulted by a dead guy more than anything.

CHAPTER 1

PUNK

F I DIDN'T NEED IT TO LOOK LIKE A SUICIDE, I WOULD'VE STRANGLED him before I pushed him. But I'm not going to let anything blow back on *her*.

I don't take my glow-in-the-dark mask off until I'm back inside my penthouse. I throw my keys on the granite counter, head straight for the fridge, and take out a bottle of ice-cold water. I press it to my forehead before opening it and taking a swig.

Fuck. I haven't felt this alive in years. But I'm angry with myself. I shouldn't have lost her in the crowd. The only joy I take is knowing that fucking pervert will never lay a hand on her again.

If I hadn't checked the back door in time… Roxy Luna would've been violated by that pig. More than she already was.

I spotted her the second she walked into Joystick tonight. Fucking gorgeous. Dark, wavy hair, sexy curves, and soft lips I want wrapped around my cock. It didn't take much to get those two idiots to tell me her name and gamertag when I went by her work a few months ago. I'll have to do something about them too. I can't have anyone else getting easy access to her.

It's been a while since I've fixated on anything other than pain meds. My therapist would call this unhealthy, but I think it's a breakthrough. I haven't been interested in pussy since before rehab three years ago. Even my sponsor might think I'm spiraling again, replacing one addiction with another.

I know all the lingo. All the fucking tactics they try to use to keep me in check. But this new high is different. It's the kind that makes me hungry for more than just rubbing one out in the shower. Roxy is perfection. From her throaty laugh all the way down to her fuck-me sneaker wedges. *And* she's a fucking gamer. She's mine. All mine.

The second she pushed past me crying, and I turned to see that disgusting piece of shit with his zipper down, I decided in that moment he had to die. The look in his eyes when he realized what I was about to do, it made me so fucking hard. I came in my pants when his body splattered on the cement below. If anyone so much as cuts my girl off in traffic, they'll end up like him.

Roxy is mine to look after, to protect, and to guide. She needs someone like me to show her how to truly be free. The friends she currently has have done a shit job. Which, speaking of…

I power up my console and send off a quick friend request to BratBaby, Roxy's blonde friend from the bar. I need her to bring me into their little gamer crew. That way, no one will suspect who I'm really after.

People think they know who I am online, but they don't have a fucking clue. No one knows that ComeFindJack11 is also me—Punk

Wilder, skateboarding legend turned degenerate. My gamertag has almost become more famous than my real-life persona.

After the fall, I had to recreate myself. I guess I'm addicted to the fame. To the accolades. If I hadn't fucked everything up that night… I'd still have my sponsors, my family's support, and my fucking dignity.

I glare up at the broken skateboard I have mounted above the fireplace. I keep it as a reminder. A warning to not let myself lose control again. My fingers shake around the controller as the memory of sirens and screams replay in my head.

My leg healed well enough so that I don't walk with a limp. But I'll never skate again. Not like before. So I threw myself into online gaming. It's the only place I can be anonymous and famous at the same time. I can still get my fix. If they only knew who hid behind the mask… they might not take too kindly to playing with me.

An alert pops up on my screen. *BratBaby has accepted your friend request.* Here we fucking go. I load into *After: 8113* and jump into the server she's in. The thought of being one step closer to Roxy makes my palms sweat and my stomach do little flips.

I have to hear her voice again. I want to know every fucking thing about her. When I check the game dashboard, I see that BratBaby is already in a session with two other names I don't recognize. I pull my hoodie up around my dirty-blond waves, disappointed.

"Wait. Hold on. There you are, baby girl." My cock twitches when I see her name pop up. JillChick22. My beautiful obsession is about to meet her match.

I power up my headset and send a request to join their private group chat. My fingers tingle as I wait. I wish I could see the looks on their faces when they see my name pop up. I can only imagine the gasps and chatter between them right now. I almost never play with a team, preferring to charge through the apocalyptic landscape solo.

Within minutes of spawning in, I'm flooded with hundreds of random requests. I'm the one who other players have wet dreams about. Any of them would kill to play with me. But ComeFindJack11 only has eyes for JillChick22 tonight.

I know BratBaby has accepted when my headset is suddenly filled with giggles and banter.

Someone says, "Shhh, shut the fuck up. He's here."

I smile and lick my lips. "How's it going, ladies?"

"Hi!" a girl shrieks.

"What's up, bro?" a dude says.

"Welcome," another guy adds.

"And dudes," I say through a laugh.

Okay, time to figure everyone out.

"Thanks for the follow." BratBaby—a.k.a. Juniper Lyons. Check.

"For sure. A friend of mine told me you guys play a lot. I've been having a hard time finding a team that can hang with me," I lie.

More giggling ensues. This is too fucking easy.

I spawn my character over to the part of the map that theirs are at. "You can call me Jack, by the way."

"Hi, Jack. Everyone here calls me Jill." Her voice is smokier than I remember. Plus, it was so loud in the bar that I didn't catch all the nuances or the depth of the rasp in it. I'm impressed she's still up playing despite the pig who assaulted her earlier tonight.

I notice her character level is thousands below mine. I doubt she has any decent weapons or shield packs. "Come stand over here, Jill. I have something for you."

I watch her avatar move across the screen, my heart racing, wishing I could physically be in the game just to be next to her. I already love how she responds to me. I can't wait to see what else I can make her do.

She picks up the package I drop for her and sighs. "Oh, I've been wanting one of these forever. Thanks, Jack."

"Anytime." I drop a couple of things for BratBaby, Skat, and RageMachine as well, so I don't look like I'm playing favorites. Or only giving gifts to the female players. There's a code of conduct online. I don't want them to think I'm some perv who just joined their group to get to the chicks. Just one chick. *My chick.*

By the time the sun is coming up outside, this entire crew is in awe of me. We make plans to play again, and they all friend request me before we log off. But the one from JillChick22 is the one I accept first. I need to play it slow though. She seems guarded and a little shy.

I can't fucking wait to break her and mold her back together the way I want. She's meant for so much more. And once I have her eating out of the palm of my hand, she won't know who the fuck she is without me.

CHAPTER 2

ROXY

I DIED. FUCK. *NOT AGAIN.*

"Anyone have an extra health pack?"

"Um, are we not going to talk about how ComeFindJack11 joined our crew last night?" Juniper calls out as her avatar drops a care package for mine.

"He's overrated," Skat grumbles.

"Ha, you're just jealous," I snort.

RageMachine chuckles. "Hell yeah, we are. You two were creaming your fucking pants when he joined."

"Gross, Rage. But you're not wrong," Juniper teases.

I feel a blush sweep across my face. ComeFindJack11 is one of the most well-known players in gaming. He seemingly came out of nowhere a few months ago. It's baffling that he'd want to play with us. Not that we suck, but we're nowhere near his level. And then hearing his voice… Fuck.

He sounded sexy, but voices can be deceiving. I once agreed to go on a date with someone I met on here and was severely disappointed. He was ten years older than he claimed to be and missing half his teeth. Never again.

But Jack… I want to imagine that he looks like a thirst trap with abs, like one of those Ghostface cosplayers. At least I can have the fantasy to get me through my dreary existence.

"Hey, you girls okay? We heard about what happened at Joystick. You didn't mention it last night," RageMachine asks. While we actually do know each other's real names, we still call each other by our gamertags on here. Skat's real name is Laken and RageMachine is really Kole.

"Yup. It happened after we left," Juniper quips.

I breathe a sigh of relief that she didn't tell them anything. "Yeah, we just found out about it today," I add. I don't like lying to my friends, but I don't have the stomach to deal with the questions that would ensue if they knew the real story.

"I feel bad for the poor girl he assaulted. But I bet she feels safer now knowing he's dead." Skat snickers.

My stomach knots. Do I feel safer? Or relieved? A twinge of guilt twists in my gut because what I really feel is joy. Pure fucking joy knowing that fucker was splattered on the pavement. That must make me a disturbed individual. I still find it hard to believe he killed himself. But what other explanation is there? No one saw what he did to me. And even if someone did, I doubt they would risk their own freedom to kill for a girl they never met.

"Okay, subject change, please," Juniper hisses. "No more talk of dead guys."

I sigh again. I'm lucky she's got my back. I'm too polite for my own good. "Sounds good to me."

We play for a few more hours until everyone starts yawning. Skat and RageMachine both have to be up early for work tomorrow. I hang back with Juniper for a few more minutes after the other two leave the group chat.

"Are you really okay, Roxy?"

I'm in shock and still processing. I don't want to think about what could've happened if that door hadn't burst open.

I take a swig of my wine. "I'm fine. I want to pretend like it never happened. Because nothing really did happen."

She sighs loudly into her headset. "Okay, Roxy. I'm here if you ever want to talk about it though."

"I know," I murmur.

"Well, I gotta cut out too. Milo called in sick, so they've got me opening the record store tomorrow," she huffs out.

"It's all good, babe. I'm going to finish up a couple of quests and head to bed soon too. I'll bring you a coffee tomorrow, and we can talk shit about Milo in front of Coast."

"That's why you're my bestie. Love you, girlie."

"Love you too."

I pour another glass of wine and sink farther into my couch cushions. I have my headset halfway off when a new notification pops up on my screen.

ComeFindJack11 is inviting you to a private group chat.

Oh, shit. I swallow down a big gulp of wine. My belly flutters. He intimidates the fuck out of me. "Fuck it." I blow out a deep breath and accept the invite.

"You left me hanging there for a minute," Jack drawls.

"Sorry," I say through a nervous chuckle. "I was getting something to drink."

"Oh, yeah? What are you drinking tonight, Jill?"

Fuck. His fucking voice. He should be narrating smutty audiobooks. "Nothing good. Just some cheap white wine."

"Mmm. A good buddy of mine owns a winery. I'll have to get you a bottle sometime. It's the good stuff."

The heat in my body rises. "Yeah, sure. Maybe." Part of me is intrigued. But then I remember he's a stranger on the internet. He could be a stalker or a serial killer.

"Relax, Jill. I'm not trying to get your address… yet." His laugh is deep and smoky.

"Very funny," I quip back. "So, what are you doing up so late?"

His avatar spawns into my location and circles mine. "I don't sleep much. And you? What's your excuse?"

"Same. And tomorrow's my day off, so I can sleep in. Lucky for you, I'm an insomniac." I grab the bottle off the kitchen counter and pour more wine. Something about him makes me want to feel light and dizzy. I haven't flirted with a man in a while.

He laughs again. "Yeah, it is. I'm glad I caught you before you logged off. Now I'm gonna keep you up all fucking night."

A tingle flickers between my thighs. I press my legs together and clench. "So sure of yourself, aren't you."

"Mmm. I always get what I want," he rasps.

Good lord. I stifle a whimper. "We'll see about that."

He chuckles, and I can guarantee there's a smirk on his face. Which is crazy because I have no idea what he looks like.

"You got plans with your boyfriend tomorrow, Jilly girl?"

Now it's my turn to smirk. I feel my cheeks flush. "Ah, fishing, are we?"

"Am I wrong to assume that a girl with a voice as sexy as yours is taken?" His voice deepens; his breaths heavier.

We aren't even playing the game anymore. Our avatars stand next to each other, unmoving.

I let out a shaky laugh. "You would be wrong to assume, yes. I am very single." Why did I say it like that? Oh, my god. Now he's going to think I'm desperate. Fuck me.

"That's a shame. Such a waste of a voice. Any man would be lucky to hear you screaming out his name in the middle of the night."

Fucking hell. I can't see myself, but I'm assuming my cheeks are bright red by the level of heat in them. "Thanks. I think."

"You're welcome. Now, let's get this character of yours leveled up. Come over here, Jill. I'm going to drop some more weapons for you. Yeah, right there. Now pick that up."

The way he commands me to him. It's just a game, but holy hell. I've never considered myself to be a sub, but I like the way he tells me what to do. There's just something satisfying about it.

"Good. Now equip the shotgun, and let's go kill some fucking swamp creatures." He spawns out, and I follow him. *Like a total fucking simp.*

We plow through the swamp, taking out toad-looking creatures left and right. I follow close behind him, his character leading the way.

"Oh, shit. I'm cornered!" I shout.

"I got you. Hang tight." Jack's avatar leaps into the middle of the group surrounding me and takes them all out with one continuous spray of bullets.

My health meter hangs by one bar. "Fuck. That was close. Thanks for the assist."

"You never have to worry about dying when I'm around, pretty girl."

A chill snakes up my back. Pretty girl. He must be referring to my avatar. It's an odd choice of words. But he's charming as fuck. "You don't know if I'm pretty."

He chuckles. "With a voice like yours, I'm sure you're a fucking knockout."

The hairs on my arms prickle. *I'm aroused by his voice.* Like fully fucking turned on. Is he aroused by mine? "I'm sure you'd like to know…" I tease.

"Come here, Jill. I have another health pack for you."

I look around the screen to see where his avatar disappeared to. "Where are you?" I laugh.

"Over there. Behind the shack. Go fetch."

I take another big gulp of wine. There's a darker tone to his voice that makes my pussy clench. It's almost degrading. *Who knew I had that kink?*

"Thanks," I murmur as I retrieve the package he dropped for me.

"Do you like it when I tell you what to do?" he rasps.

I swallow down the lump in my throat, my palms sweating around my controller. I let out a nervous giggle. "I appreciate you helping me in the game."

He breathes heavily into the headset. "That's not what I asked. Do you like being submissive?"

Another tingle flickers straight to my clit. I clench my thighs tightly together, desperate to feel some kind of friction. "Um… I don't understand."

He sucks in a sharp breath. "I think you do… Let's play a different kind of game. Take off your panties."

Oh, fuck. "Excuse me? You're joking, right?" Great. He's a fucking pervert.

"I can hear the ache in your voice, Jilly girl. I'm giving you permission to relieve it. Now put your controller down and take them off."

My fingers tremble. "I don't even know you. You've got a lot of nerve asking me this."

"I'm not asking. And if you didn't want to do it, you would've already logged off and blocked me."

Fuck. He's right. I'm curious as to how far this is going to go. And I've been wet from the second I heard his voice tonight.

I set the controller down on my coffee table and chug the rest of my wine. I slide my sweatpants off first. A sigh escapes my throat at the thought of what I'm doing.

"I-I don't think I can do this." I squeak.

"You can and you will. If I have to tell you again, there will be a punishment," he growls.

Shit. Fuck. I don't even know what reality I'm in anymore. I push my black lace panties down to my ankles and kick them off.

"O-okay. They're off," I stutter.

"Good girl. Now spread your legs apart and hold your controller against your pussy."

I'm in deep and too far to turn back now. Sober and hungover me is going to hate *this* me in the morning.

I open my legs and press the controller against my clit. "Okay," I say on a shaky breath. "What now?" *I feel so naughty.*

He actually purrs. "Now, I'm going to take your character to the edge of death, heal her, then do it again. Over and over until I hear you cum."

The controller vibrates when you're being attacked in the game.

Fucking hell. But after everything that happened last night at Joystick, this makes me feel more in control than I've ever felt. Last night, I was helpless.

Just like the day I tore my ACL. It was my fault I didn't land the switch leap. I knew it seconds before my feet hit the ground. It was the aftermath I lost control of. Losing my scholarship, my dance partner, and even my boyfriend. I gave up.

At this moment, I just want to feel something other than my own bitter apathy. I want to feel alive.

I take a deep breath and lean back against the couch.

"Don't take your eyes off the screen. I want you to watch how I get you off," he commands.

He fires the first round of shots at my avatar. The sudden vibration of the controller sends a spasm to my clit. I bite my lip to stifle a moan. Sweat beads down my back.

"I can hear you suppressing what you want. I don't like that. Moan for me, or I'll edge you all fucking night." He fires off another round of shots, and I gasp.

"Fuck," I whine as I arch my back, pressing my hips farther into the couch cushions.

"Mmm. Better. Do you like how I can touch you without even being in the same room?"

I never thought of it that way. Fuck. I'm even more turned on now. "We don't even know each other," I rasp. I lick a bead of sweat off my upper lip.

"We're getting to know each other real good tonight. I'm learning all the right buttons to press." He loads a max-capacity clip into his machine gun and fires off a longer round. A deep moan belts from my throat as my body shakes, my toes curling. The vibration sends shockwaves through my core.

"Please," I beg. "Stop." There are no intelligible thoughts in my head. I'm spiraling, teetering back and forth between desire and shame.

He chuckles. "You can move the controller anytime you want. Only you can make this stop. Because I won't."

I exhale slowly, my teeth chattering as the controller reverberates through me. "No, let's keep going."

"I had a feeling you might say that."

He fires off another long round of gunshots at my avatar, and I buck.

"*Fuuck.*"

CHAPTER 3

PUNK

"**L**IE DOWN ON YOUR COFFEE TABLE, REST THE CONTROLLER ON your pussy, and put your hands above your head." I have to fight the urge to go to her apartment, break down her door, and take what's mine. It's too soon. She's not ready. But the sound of her whimpering has my cock so fucking hard that I can barely breathe.

I hear her clearing off her table, her breaths shallow. Roxy is easier to dominate than I thought she would be. Easier to control and manipulate. She's been neglected for so long it didn't take much to get her panties off. I only wish I could see how her pussy glistens for me.

"O-okay. I'm lying down. I don't know why I'm doing this…" she murmurs the last part.

"Because you like being my little doll. You like me positioning you the way I want. It makes your skin hot and your cunt wet."

"Fuck," she whispers.

"If I was there with you, your wrists would be tied. And it would be my tongue making you fall apart." I unzip my pants and set my cock free. I'm so close to bursting. But I want us to cum at the same time.

She whimpers again. "You would tie me up?"

"Mmm. I would. You'd like that. I bet you wish you were tied up right now." I stroke my shaft, imagining all the ways I would confine her and bind her so she could never get away.

"I've never been tied up, so I don't know." The ache in her voice is killing me. Fucking hell. I will be the first man to do these vile things to her. She'll beg for her freedom. For her sanity. But I won't give it to her until she's foaming at the mouth. And then I'll be her savior. She'll be so grateful for the release that she'll do anything I tell her to.

"I think you do know. The idea of it is making you so fucking hot, isn't it? Don't lie to me, pretty girl. I'll know."

She whimpers again. "I've fantasized about it before..."

I know her fantasies better than she does. Fucking hell. "Look at the screen, Jilly girl. Do you see what I'm holding?"

"Oh, fuck. Yes."

I aim the auto grenade launcher at her avatar. "I want to hear you scream when you cum. That's the payment you owe me."

I can tell she's shaking by the quickness of her breath. "Please... I'm so close."

A sadistic chuckle flutters out of me as I press the trigger. A flurry of grenades assaults her avatar without relief.

She gasps and cries out. I hear something smack against her table. Fuck. "I'm cumming..." she squeals.

"Mmm, thatta girl. Talk to me. How much cum are you spilling

26

for me?" I stroke my cock faster, the blood rushing to the tip. I squeeze my pre cum out and roll my thumb through it.

"It-it came out fast… Fuck, that's never happened before," she cries.

Damn, I need to be in that apartment. I pump my cock harder. "Did you squirt for me, pretty girl?"

"Yes," she whines.

Fuck. I wish I could lick her clean. "You made a mess, didn't you?"

Her breath is erratic. "It's all over my table."

I bite my lip as a spasm rushes down my shaft. I grit my teeth. *She can't hear me cum.* Not this time. I jerk and shake as an orgasm shatters me. I roll my hips off the couch and cum into my palm.

"Lick it off."

She gasps. "What? I'm not doing that."

I keep stroking my shaft with my left hand while my cum still pools out into my right palm. "Do it. Get on your hands and knees… and clean up your fucking mess."

I bite my lip so hard that blood fills my mouth. I can hear her shifting around again, obeying my every command.

"No. I can't do this. It's disgusting." She groans.

I lick my lips, relishing the taste of my own blood. "You took too long to take off your panties. This is your punishment. Do it, or you'll never hear from me again."

My heart races to see what she's going to do. If she'll call my bluff. I have no intention of letting this creature ever get away from me. But she doesn't know that… yet.

I hear her groan again and then whine. "Fine."

A sick pleasure rolls through me as I hear her tongue slop up her own cum off the table. She whimpers the whole time. But I'd bet my entire penthouse that she's wet again. She licks for longer than I anticipated, which makes me fucking hard again. *How much did she cum?*

"There. I did it. All clean," she snaps.

I bite back a chuckle. Now I know for sure I can get her to do anything I want. She's mine. "Thatta girl. Now go get some sleep. But don't even think about putting those panties back on. I want you to remember me between your legs all night long."

She breathes heavily into the headset. "Um, Jack… what the fuck just happened?"

"Nothing happened, Jilly girl. We played a fun game tonight. I got you leveled up a few more times. And you repaid me for it. Relax and go to bed now."

"Whatever," she mutters. "Goodnight, Jack."

I chuckle and log off without another word. I lie back and get myself off again while I imagine her lying in bed without panties. I have her. She's going to bend and break to my will. Tonight proved that. And I can't wait to see how far I can get her to go.

CHAPTER 4

ROXY

IN THE TIME IT TAKES ME TO ORDER TWO LATTES, WAIT FOR THEM TO be made, and for me to carry them into Vinyl Delights, I decide I'm not going to tell Juniper anything about last night. Not even that Jack and I played *After: 8113* together. *Jack.* I wonder what his real name is.

"Did you have a booty call last night? You're glowing." Juniper takes one of the lattes from me.

I bite my lip and look away, willing myself not to blush. "Nope. I used a new face mask."

"Liar." She pinches my arm. "You fucked someone last night."

I sigh. "Okay fine. I didn't get a new face mask. I got a new vibrator." Technically, I'm not completely lying to my best friend. Just omitting some crucial details.

Her face falls. "Oh. Boo. I was hoping you finally got a real cock between your legs."

I roll my eyes at her. "Sorry to disappoint."

"But what's the name of that vibrator? You're like seriously glowing," she half-teases.

I send her the link to a vibrator that I don't in fact own. And then add it to my cart as well. Juniper is the kind of friend who will ask to look at it when she comes over next. Just to make sure it's the size and color she wants. It's exhausting keeping up with her sometimes.

She snickers when Coast walks by, trying to eavesdrop. "How's your friend's dick? I heard he fell on it when he was jerking off."

A spurt of coffee dribbles out as I try to contain my laughter. "*Juniper*. You're so fucking mean."

"He has a cold," he grumbles under his breath.

She bursts out laughing. "What? I bet I'm right."

I shake my head. "Your mouth is going to get you in trouble one of these days."

She winks and takes another sip of her latte. "My mouth likes trouble."

If only she knew what I did last night. She'd probably be proud of me. I took a page straight out of her book. But I'm not the girl who lets strangers on the internet make her cum. Have I been so deprived that I jump at the first opportunity?

"You're blushing. Are you sure you didn't hook up with any-one last night?" She eyes me like a hawk, searching my face for any signs of weakness.

"No. I promise you. I didn't." Technically, not another lie. I did not hook up with Jack. She doesn't need to know that I let him get me off with my controller.

Satisfied that I'm telling the truth, she looks back toward Coast. "I'm going to have so much fun fucking with him all day."

I laugh and pull her in for a side hug. "All right, I'm gonna get out of here. Hanging out at your job on your day off should be a crime."

"You playing tonight?" she asks.

I bite my lip. If I say no, then she'll definitely know something's up. I nod. "Yeah, for sure. I'll be on later."

She blows me a kiss and sets her sights back on Coast. Poor guy. It's a wonder he hasn't quit yet.

I freeze when I get to my car. The passenger side door is wide open. *What the fuck?*

I glance around to see if anyone's lurking. Satisfied that I'm not being watched, I inch forward. A chill snakes up my neck when I peer inside. There's a flyer from Joystick on my passenger seat. The one Vinyl Delights sent out for the party the other night. *That wasn't there earlier, was it?*

My stomach knots. I suddenly feel like I'm being messed with. *Did someone else see what happened to me that night?* I crumple up the flyer and throw it in the back. I'm shaking by the time I slide into the driver's seat and lock the doors.

I take deep breaths as a panic attack threatens to surface. Maybe it was my flyer that I just forgot to throw away. And I could have easily left the door open when I grabbed the carry tray with our lattes off the seat.

I'm just being fucking paranoid. I need to stop. And yet I can't help glancing in the rearview mirror every two minutes the entire drive home.

"Bro, Godzilla would annihilate Dracula. No question."

"You're drunk. No fucking way. Dracula would eat Godzilla for fucking breakfast," Skat snaps at RageMachine.

I laugh as I log into the group chat. "We've already established this. Even *if* Dracula managed to sink his fangs into Godzilla, he'd never be able to drain him fast enough."

"One hundred percent," Juniper quips. "Listen to Jilly, boys. She knows her monsters."

"Oh yeah? So, who's your favorite monster?" Jack rasps.

His voice jars me. I didn't notice him log in. I swallow down the nervous lump in my throat. "Frankenstein's monster, of course."

"That's weak, Jilly," RageMachine says.

Jack chuckles. "Tell me why."

There he goes again. It's the demanding tone in his voice that no one seems to catch but me.

I clear my throat. "Because he's not really a monster at all. He didn't choose to exist. The townspeople vilified him for being different. But he never meant to scare anyone."

"So you like misunderstood villains? You think you can save them with that sweet spot between your legs?" Jack asks.

"Whoa! Welcome to the party, Jack," Juniper shrieks.

The heat in my chest rises. He's antagonizing me. Pushing my buttons. "You can't save anyone who doesn't want to be. And I certainly would never confuse sex with compassion."

"So you're saying you don't want to fuck Frankenstein?" Skat chimes in. "I thought you girls like monster cock."

Juniper cackles. "I'd fuck Frankenstein."

I white-knuckle my controller. "Frankenstein is the doctor, *not* the monster. Anyway, it doesn't matter. Godzilla would destroy Dracula. And you're all dumb as hell."

Laughter erupts.

I'm seething. Even Juniper is pissing me off tonight. I usually don't get riled up by their teasing. It's Jack who's winding me up.

"Hey, Jilly, I'm just fucking with you. Relax for me," Jack coos.

I shudder. His commands are subtle to everyone else, but for me… they're a trigger. The memory of the controller vibrating between my thighs sends a wave of tingles through my core.

"I know. It's all good." I force myself to say it in a lighter tone.

I go through the motions, following them around the swampland while they continue to roast each other. The more I listen to his voice, the more feral I get. My body and mind are in opposition to each other. I've never let anyone degrade me like this before.

"All right, guys. I'm heading to bed. I'm working early in the morning," I say on a fake yawn.

Juniper snorts. "You work at ten tomorrow."

My cheeks burn. I fire a shot at her avatar. "Oops, sorry." She must be drunker than usual if she's not catching my hints.

"Stay and play for another hour, Jilly girl," Jack says. It's not a plea but another demand.

"Nope. I have to go. Goodnight, everyone." I log off and power down my headset before anyone can respond.

Juniper sends me a text message. *You okay?*

I blow out a deep breath. I guess I'm not. The incident with ComeFindJack11 has me more on edge than I thought. It's making me question my own morals. I wanted him to keep going. *I came so fucking hard I squirted.* And then I licked it off my coffee table. The shame threatens to choke me unconscious.

I fire off a quick text. One that I know will shut her up real quick. *Yeah, sorry. I just started my period.*

Another lie to my best friend. Ugh. Fuck.

She responds back at lightspeed. *Enough said. Wash down a couple of pills with some whiskey and curl up with the heating pad. I'll stop by the store tomorrow and check on you.*

My gaming console pings with a flurry of messages. Fuck. I open the message center to see they're all from Jack.

I hope I didn't upset you tonight, pretty girl.

Why is it so hot when he calls me that?

The next message is a link to an article titled: *Frankenstein's Monster—the most misunderstood creature in Victorian Literature.*

That makes me chuckle. "Asshole," I mutter through a smirk.

I flip to the third message, and my grin widens.

I'll let you off the hook tonight. But tomorrow, we're back on. Just you and me.

But it's the fourth and final message that shatters me…

Fetch yourself a pair of nipple clamps tomorrow. Make sure you have them on when you log back in.

Holy fuck. I'm playing a dangerous game with this man. One with far greater consequences than the one our avatars run around in. But I can't help but get excited about what he's going to tell me to do next. It's like discovering a new drug for the first time. A new addiction with the highest highs and lowest of lows.

My ex wouldn't dream of talking to me this way. We fucked in the missionary position on most nights, with the occasional doggy style when he was black-out drunk. He cringed at the sight of my vibrator and didn't understand the beauty of self-pleasure. Which was a shame because it was the only way I could cum most of the time.

And then along comes Jack with his sexy voice and his carnal demands. I'm quickly succumbing to his every fucked-up whim. Maybe this is the best thing for me. We don't know each other's real names or faces. There's no way to get attached. It's the perfect situation. And when either of us gets tired of it, we'll walk away. We'll just log off.

I send a quick reply back before going to bed. *I already own nipple clamps.*

CHAPTER 5

PUNK

MY LITTLE OBSESSION HAS A TOY FETISH. SHE'S NOT AS innocent as I first thought. I chuckle as I reread her message back in the app that links to my console. *I already own nipple clamps.*

I pull my baseball cap down low and flip the hood of my sweatshirt over it before walking into the coffee shop. I spot her dark-brown hair hanging down the curve of her back. She stands with her ankles crossed, in baggy jeans and a form-fitting purple hoodie, unaware of her own sex appeal.

I keep my head down when I approach the counter. "Large black coffee, please."

Roxy waits for her drink at the pickup counter, her head buried in her phone, oblivious to me watching her. Completely clueless to the fact that she's my prey, ripe for the slaughter. I bet she's pretty when she cries too. I can't wait to see tears streaming down her cheeks when I fuck her throat raw.

The blonde cashier's eyes widen when she hands me my coffee. "Aren't you Punk Wilder?"

I wink and put my fingers to my lips. "Shhh."

She blushes and nods before turning to the redhead steaming milk. They whisper and stare as I walk toward the condiment counter to grab a lid and a cup sleeve. This is the reason I don't go out in public often.

I'm lucky that these girls are fans. Usually, I get cursed out by Gen-X parents, furious with me for ruining the image of their kids' idol. I just wanted to skate. *I never signed up to be a fucking hero.*

I lean against the window and watch as Roxy flashes the barista a massive smile when she places the latte in front of her. "Thanks, girl."

It didn't take long for me to track her down. There are only three coffee shops within close proximity to Vinyl Delights. BratBaby, a.k.a. Juniper, was dumb enough to announce that Roxy works at ten this morning. So I was able to get a head start.

The process of elimination was easy. The closest one to her work is a big chain coffee shop with questionable associations and shitty coffee. Roxy doesn't seem like the type to give money to places like that. The second shop is so bougie that the cheapest latte goes for seven dollars. And that's just for a small. That's half her hourly wage at the record store.

Which brings me to spot number three. Pick Your Poison—a funky little hipster café just three blocks away from Vinyl Delights. She arrived promptly at 9:30 a.m., as I predicted. That gives her thirty minutes to take her time and enjoy her drink on the walk back over.

I turn my back and step to the side as she approaches the condiment bar. She still pays me no attention as she fiddles with her lid and cup sleeve. Roxy needs to learn how to be more aware of her surroundings. I can't let what happened to her at Joystick transpire again. It was too close. Lucky for her, I came along when I did. Now she has me looking out for her.

I catch a whiff of something sweet like peaches and cream. My mouth salivates. I want to lick every inch of her skin. Mmm, my fragile little bud. *I can't wait to brutalize you*. I'm going to make her stronger, tougher, and wild as the fucking weeds that ravage the sidewalks of Lavender Heights.

The squeak of her sneakers across the linoleum floor serves as my cue. I count to ten while I wait for her to pass through the door. Once the cool draft caresses my cheeks, I'm on the move again.

At six foot three, I'm anything but inconspicuous. But I keep my head down with one eye trained on the swish of Roxy's hips. I follow her for three blocks until we reach the record store.

I lurk near her car. The same one I broke into the other day. Leaving the Joystick flyer on her seat was fucked up, but I need to see just how fragile she is. I watched her from afar, waiting to see how she'd break. But she didn't show any emotion on her face. She held her composure. I had to resist the urge to follow her home. To see her crumble in the safety of her own space. But I can't risk her discovery until I'm ready.

Stalking her is my foreplay. I've never found anyone worthy of hunting before her. This is a new kink for me. I hadn't meant to stay hidden that night at the arcade, but following her in the shadows made me so fucking hard. It's a game I want to keep playing.

My heart races when I spot the dude who's been coming in

here every day this week. On Roxy's days off, he leaves without buying anything or even browsing. But when she's here… he stays for hours, chatting her ear off. This jersey-wearing troll is short, stocky, and drives one of those lifted trucks with a sticker on the back that says *Go Wolves*.

He was the jock in high school who shit on skaters and thought football was king. I knew so many assholes like him. The kind who thought they were better than me. They think skateboarding isn't even a real sport. Until the day these douchebags find out they're nowhere near good enough for the NFL, while I end up traveling the world making millions of dollars in sponsor deals. *Who's the mother fucking king now?*

I watch as he makes a direct line for Roxy. She smiles politely, of course. She's too fucking nice. I come out of my skin when he pats her arm. Fucking hell. Sweat beads on my forehead. She's mine. How fucking dare he? No one should be touching her but me. Now his filth is on her.

I grit my teeth when she throws her head back and laughs at something he says. *Fucking hold it together, Punk, or you'll ruin everything.* But I feel more alive than ever. More clear and focused. Who needs drugs when you have pure fucking rage? It's like no other high I've ever known. And I'm addicted to it.

I release a shaky breath when that piece of shit finally leaves the store. As much as I want to stay and watch my girl through the window, it's more important to eliminate this new threat. He wants to do vile things to her, just like the man I pushed off the roof of Joystick. But this time, I'm going to take care of it before he even gets a chance to corner her.

This fucking dude. Imma call him Bryce. He looks like a fucking Bryce. With pop-punk music bumping from his speakers over the engorged exhaust of his stupid truck, this fucker has no clue that I've been tailing him all day.

He paid two hundred and thirty-seven dollars to fill up his monstrous gas tank after scarfing down an entire bag of cheese-dusted chips and a diet soda. Fucking disgusting. I'm up every morning at five—shower, gym, shower again, green drink and acai bowl for breakfast, plain chicken breast and water for lunch, then steak and sparkling water for dinner.

My body is a sculpted fucking temple. One that Roxy is going to worship very soon. And to think he touched her with those same grubby hands. My cock twitches as I fantasize about choking him with the beef jerky stick he didn't finish.

We're back in motion again, driving aimlessly through Lavender Heights. It's like he's trying to waste time *and* all that fucking expensive gas he just filled up on. I tighten my grip around the handlebars of my bike, growing more impatient by the second as the engine rattles the flesh on my thighs. The hum usually soothes me. But my craving to spill blood consumes me. I need another hit before I explode.

I hoped to go back to the record store and watch Roxy close up, but this fool hasn't stopped long enough for me to get a hold of him. I hang back farther now, careful not to alert him. I check the tracker on my phone when I stop at the red light. He's about six blocks away, heading toward the industrial district.

I managed to tag the underside of his truck when he stopped for gas. One of the perks of being a millionaire. I have lots of cool fucking gadgets. I switch tracker profiles and see that Roxy's car is still parked in front of Vinyl Delights. I check the time on my phone. Fuck. It's 6:30 p.m. She's going to be clocking out soon.

I hit the throttle and continue tracking Bryce. After a few more miles, he leads me toward a cul-de-sac in the seedier part of town. Perfect. No one gives a fuck about their neighbors here. I kill the engine a few blocks away. I take off my helmet and replace it with a black surgical mask. People can think I'm a germaphobe or some shit. And it's less suspicious than the glow-in-the-dark one I like to wear to parties. I pull my hood up over my head and creep in his direction on foot.

He stumbles out of his truck and slams the driver's door shut, leaving cheese-dusted fingerprints on the shiny black paint. *Is this fucker drunk?* I glance inside the truck to see an empty bottle of vodka on the passenger seat. I chuckle. I'm doing the world a fucking favor.

As Bryce lumbers up the stairs to his apartment, I glance around to make sure no one's paying attention. I spot an old lady shutting her blinds in the house across the street. It's dark, and I'm wearing all black. There's no way she'd ever be able to place me. Not to mention she doesn't fucking care. People tend to mind their business in this part of town.

When I reach his door, it's wide open. It's like the universe wants me to kill this guy. I step in and shut it quietly behind me. I also lock it just in case he has any buddies who are planning on stopping by.

I hear a crash and head toward it, finding myself in his mess of a kitchen. Dirty dishes pile up in the sink, the trash overflows onto the floor, and flies buzz around a half-eaten burger that looks like it's been there for days. Bryce pops up from the open fridge with a beer in his hand.

"What the fuuck?" he slurs. "Who-who is you?"

Fucking hell. He can't even speak properly. "Oh, Bryce. *Look* at this shithole. You really are a disgusting pig." I wave my hands around at the cesspool that surrounds us.

He rubs his bloodshot eyes and blinks a few times before stumbling forward. "You want a beer, man?"

"I don't drink," I grit out. *Not anymore.*

"Wells, what the fuck you want?" He loses his footing and wobbles to the side, smacking into the kitchen counter.

"I'm here to kill you. You shouldn't have touched my girl, Bryce." I remove the hunting knife from my jacket pocket and inch toward him.

His eyes glaze. "Who da hell is Bryyyce?" he slurs.

I chuckle. "That's the name I give all douchebags. Isn't that what you are, Bryce?"

He licks his lips and tilts his head. "Yeah. So? I'm drafted. I'm going there. To the football place."

Holy fuck, this man is obliterated. He's so pathetic I can't stand to look at him anymore. "No, buddy. You're not. You're a thirty-five-year-old out of shape drunk who likes preying on young pretty girls."

"Hey, fuck you."

I grin beneath my mask. "Shhh, it's time."

He doesn't notice the knife until it's plunging into him. He gasps and looks down. "You stabbed me. Fuck."

I cover his mouth with my gloved hand. "I am extremely protective of my girl. I can't allow you to get away with putting your filthy hands on her."

I press my forearm into his neck and pin him to the counter while he flails against me. He's top-heavy, but I'm stronger than him. My knee might be fucked up, but the rest of me is hard, lean muscle. I twist the knife in his gut and pull up, splitting him open from belly button to nipple.

His cries are gargled. He shakes violently in my grasp. Blood gushes from his torso, coating the linoleum as it pools at our feet.

"That's it. Let it all go," I coax.

His pulse slows along with his breath. I count to ten and pull out the knife. His eyes roll back, and his body goes slack. As soon as I step back, he slumps to the floor.

I let out a deep breath. "You should've gone to a different record store, buddy."

I rinse off my knife in the sink, careful not to touch any of his moldy dishes, and slip it back into my jacket. I look down at the mess I made of him and smirk. This is so much better than snorting cocaine.

As I walk out the front door, I decide to leave it wide open, as I had originally found it. The cops will assume he was drunk and forgot to close it, which is true, and that it was a robbery gone bad. On that thought, I double back in and take the cash from his wallet and the rings off his fingers.

I remove the tracker from his truck and casually walk down the street toward my bike. I let out a sigh as the engine roars to life. Another victory and one less creep trying to get at my girl. I don't care how many assholes I have to kill. Roxy belongs to me.

CHAPTER 6

ROXY

I feel ridiculous. There's no way ComeFindJack11 was being serious, right? And yet here I am, sitting on my couch in a T-shirt and sweats, wearing nipple clamps. Maybe when I fell and tore my ACL, I hit my head too. I must have fucking brain damage. What other logical reason could there be for me acting like a whore with a stranger on the internet?

I make myself a mocktail instead of an alcoholic beverage, testing myself to see if I can act like less of a slut around this man when I'm sober. Although, liquid courage would be helpful right now as I power up my console and my headset, my hands trembling around the controller.

There's a game already in session when I check the message board, finding a group invite from RageMachine. I draw in a deep breath and click on it.

"Jilly!" Juniper shrieks, always careful to call me by my gamertag when new players have joined. Jack might be the it boy of the gaming world, but he's still a stranger. I'm grateful she still has some sense about her after calling me out last night for jumping off early.

"What's up, guys? Miss me?"

Skat and RageMachine both snort at the same time and mumble something about my character slowing them down.

"There she is," Jack announces.

My belly flips, and I'm suddenly very aware of the cold metal clamps pinched around my nipples. "Hi, Jack," I say on a breath.

"Did you do that thing I told you to?" His voice is deeper tonight.

"I-I did…"

"What thing?" Juniper squeaks.

Fucking hell. I can't believe he's bringing it up already. He has no idea how nosy my friends are.

"I'll let Jilly tell you." He chuckles.

"Oh, um. It's nothing. Jack was just telling me what mods to get for the new gun he gave me." *Please fucking believe me.*

"Yeah. Exactly. Now when she *pinches* the trigger, the bullets release faster. There's way more kickback, but it's efficient." I can hear his muffled laughter. I'm going to fucking kill him.

My cheeks heat. "Yup. Thanks again."

"Oh, awesome. Have you tried it out yet?" Juniper asks.

The fact that they think we're actually talking about a weapon mod makes me want to laugh too. But he's playing a dangerous game now.

"Yeah, try it out, Jilly. *Pinch* that trigger for me." Jack snickers.

Fuck. A nervous laugh leaves my throat. "I will for sure. Later. I'm just organizing my skill box right now."

Skat and RageMachine both boo me. *For fuck's sake.*

"Show us now, Jilly." The tone in Jack's voice darkens. He's making his first demand of the night. It sends a spasm to my clit.

A private message from him pops up. *Tighten the clamps.*

Fuck. "Okay," I say out loud to the group even though I meant to type it only to him. "I mean. Yes, I'll show you the new gun mod."

Jack's avatar spawns over to my location and drops a package for me. I pick up the new gun and fast travel to the rest of my friends on the map.

"We're waiting," he grits out.

"Girl, hurry up. I have to pee," Juniper whines.

They have no fucking idea what they're asking me to do. I load the gun and press the trigger button on my controller before tightening each clamp.

Tingles surge through me. I want his mouth wrapped around my nipples, licking the metal that grips them. I want that filthy tongue of his to punish me. Fuck. A whimper escapes my lips.

"You okay?" Skat asks.

"Um, yeah. Sorry, I spilled my drink," I lie.

"How did that new trigger feel?" Jack asks, his voice thick with lust and ache.

Fuck this. I grab an empty glass and pour a healthy amount of wine into it. "Um… really good. Thank you."

He chuckles.

"Nice piece. Hey, Jack, can you give me one of those?" Juniper asks.

I almost choke on my wine.

"Sorry, BratBaby. I only had one left." He chuckles again.

Another private message from him appears on my screen. *I know this is making you hot. Take your shirt off until you cool down.*

This is insane. Why am I so excited? Fuck me. I take off my headset for a second so I can pull my T-shirt off. Now I'm sitting half-naked on my couch while I play video games with a man I've never met.

I reply back. *It's off.*

I hear him chuckle again in my headset. I'm quickly becoming his puppet. I feel like I should be more alarmed, but I'm surrendering to the role without hesitating. I'm not sure what that says about me, but at least it keeps me from going out and fucking random dudes.

When I finally look at my phone, it's almost midnight. We've been playing for five hours and I've polished off the entire bottle of wine. I'm drunk. And after listening to this man's voice for half the night, I'm horny too.

By the time we say our goodbyes and everyone starts logging off, my nipples are raw. I need to quench this ache. To feel some sort of release. Once everyone has left the group chat, Jack bursts out laughing.

"Fuck you. I'm taking these off now," I grumble. The first thing on my list after this is fucking my vibrator senseless.

"That's not how this works, pretty girl. You've submitted to me. And I don't want you to take them off yet." He's breathing heavily into his mic, aroused. "Touch them."

I lay back against my couch. Droplets of sweat bead down between my breasts. "They're too sensitive."

"Mmm, I bet they are. If I was there with you right now, I'd bite them so fucking hard, you'd scream like you were dying." There's so much rasp in his voice I wonder if he's touching himself.

I swallow down the lump in my throat. "This isn't healthy. I don't think I can do this anymore."

He chuckles. "You're pissed that I make you cum harder with

47

just my voice than any other man has ever been able to in the flesh."
He lets out a soft moan. "Yeah, I bet your last ex couldn't even find
your G-spot. Isn't that why you have so many toys, pretty girl?"

Fuck. "It's none of your business, Jack. I'm taking these off."

"Not yet. Do you own a mask, Jilly?"

My stomach flips. Halloween is my favorite holiday. I have a
whole section in my closet stocked with costumes and masks. "Yeah,
why?" I say on a shaky breath.

He purrs into his mic. "I want to see you. Put on a mask and
video chat with me before you take those clamps off."

A tiny chill snakes up my back. This is getting more dangerous. If he turns out to be a psycho, I'm playing right into his hands.
But I can't resist. I want to see him too. Even if his face is covered.

"I don't think that's a good idea, Jack."

"Don't you wanna play with me? Show me how good of a slut
you are for me."

Fucking hell. If anyone else called me that, it would be game
over. But the way he says it sends a spasm straight to my core. His
possessiveness makes me feel protected and desired.

I blow out a deep breath as I make my way to my closet in
search of a mask. We're both quiet as I scrounge through all of them
before settling on a creepy plastic baby doll face. I hate that he's quiet
because he knows I'm obeying him.

I put it on and then readjust my headset around it. Shit. Am I
really about to do a video chat with this guy I barely know? While
wearing nothing but a mask and nipple clamps? It sparks a dangerous streak in me. A fantasy I've long had and a kink I've always
wanted to explore. If it gets too weird, I'll just block him and log off.

"Okay, Jack. I'll play. The mask is on." I set up my webcam on
the coffee table, turn it on, and wait.

My stomach knots when the video chat request pops up a few minutes later. My finger hovers over the accept button as I contemplate the line I'm about to cross.

"You already said yes, Jilly. No takebacks." He snickers.

I hit accept and shudder when I see him. I can tell he's tall even though he's sitting down. He's also ripped. His broad shoulders and thick arms fill out his black hoodie. His glow-in-the-dark mask has x's over the eyes and mouth. I almost drool.

He unzips his jeans and leans back in his chair. "Jilly girl. So fucking sexy. Come closer so I can see you better."

I do as he says, mesmerized by him like he's some sort of dark internet prince. "Can I take them off now?"

He tilts his head to the side. "Yes. You've been a good girl."

As I release each clamp, a rush of blood shoots into my nipples, making them tingle and pulse. I let out a sigh of relief.

He takes out his thick cock and fists it in his gloved hand, pumping it slowly. "I want to suck and bite those perfect red buds. I bet they taste like peaches and cream."

My body wash *is* peach. Lucky guess. My mouth salivates as I watch his hand sliding up and down his shaft. I ache to taste him too. Fuck. "Tell me something about yourself, Jack."

"Get on your knees first. I want to see what you look like when I'm about to fuck your mouth," he growls.

My breath hitches. I lower myself to the floor in front of the coffee table. "What do you do for a living?"

He pinches the tip of his cock. "Shhh, open your mouth and stick out your tongue."

Fuck. "But… my mask."

"Lift it up. Let me see your pretty face."

Juices leak out from my pussy as I do what he says. This is

fucked up on so many levels. And now he knows what I look like. But I can't say no to this man. *Fuck*.

"Good girl." He pumps his cock faster, jerking his hips up and down. "Put two fingers in your mouth and gag yourself. Show me what you look like choking."

I let out a whimper as I press my fingers all the way back. I convulse and lurch forward, whimpering as I suck my own fingers.

"Oh, yeah, just like that. Mmm, I'm getting so close. I wish I could cum inside that pretty mouth."

The ache between my thighs grows. I can't help but whine and moan as I watch him jerk himself off, wishing he was right here in this room with me.

"Such a good little slut. Now take your other two fingers and slide them deep inside your pussy."

"Oh, shit." He's pulling all my strings like a marionette. I'm so fucking hot I can barely breathe. I let out a deep moan as I thrust two fingers inside my wet cunt.

"See how much better I make you? You're almost perfect, pretty girl."

The way he degrades me should be alarming, but I can't stop obeying him. It makes me feel dirty in the best way. "Please, I need to cum."

"Say my name when you beg me," he snaps.

I roll my thumb in circles around my clit. "Please, Jack. Can I cum?"

He pumps his cock hard and fast as he grunts. "Again. Make me believe you. I want to hear how badly you need this."

Fuck. The act is turning me on even more. "Please, Jack. I'm so close it hurts. I need it. Fucking hell. I need to cum. *Jack...*"

"Fuck," he grits out. "Cum. Now."

We both unleash ourselves, our moans drowning the other's out. I see his cum shoot out as mine instantly soaks my fingers.

"Thank you, Jack. I needed that…"

"You're welcome, Roxy."

I freeze, my fingers still inside my pussy. All the hairs on the back of my arms stand up. "What did you just say?"

He sighs. "I said you're welcome, Jilly."

I shake my head as he looks right at me through the webcam. "No, you called me something else. Where did you hear that name?"

He leans forward, getting closer to the screen. "You're confused. That's how hard I can make you cum. Now go get some sleep. I expect you back here for another game tomorrow night."

"Jack… I'm not confused. You called me something else. I swear it. What is going on?" I'm fully freaked out now as I pull my T-shirt back over my head, lifting the headset up through it.

"I think you've had too much to drink, pretty girl. You know that shit is bad for you, right? No alcohol tomorrow night. I want my girl sober next time she cums."

His girl? He's a psycho. Fuck. "Okay, Jack," I murmur.

"I like your mask. It suits you. My little rag doll that I get to undress and position any way I want."

Another spasm trickles to my core, and I curse myself. Every word and command out of his mouth is a trigger straight to my pussy.

"I have to go to bed now."

"Goodnight, pretty girl." He clicks off his camera and logs off.

I'm speechless. All I can do is sit here while my head explodes. I know what I heard. He called me Roxy. *How the fuck does he know my real name?*

"I swear on Jason Momoa, I never told him your real name, Rox. No one did." Juniper slips another record in between two others. One of our regulars just dropped off another box of vinyl he found at a garage sale.

"Well, then what the fuck? This is really starting to creep me out." I chew on the straw of my iced latte.

She snickers. "Why were you on with him after we all logged off anyway? It's giving secret love affair vibes."

My cheeks heat. Fuck. "Um. He's just been helping me with a few things in the game."

"Bullshit," she says through a snort. "Your face is as red as this album cover. Spill the fucking tea, bestie." She holds up a copy of "Rebel Yell" by Billy Idol.

I have been feeling so fucking guilty for keeping this from her. "It's nothing. We've flirted a little."

She sets the stack down and arches an eyebrow at me. "You're a terrible liar."

I blow out a deep sigh. "Fine. He sometimes gets me off. Like we talk dirty to each other."

Her mouth drops open. "You're having headset sex with ComeFindJack11?"

"Shhh." I glance around the store to see both of our customers gawking in our direction. "It's not sex. Well, it kind of is. He makes me do things…"

Her grin widens. "Ooh, you dirty little slut. What kinds of things?"

I grab her wrist and yank her in the back. "Milo, can you watch the front for us?"

He looks at me like a deer caught in the headlights. "Everything okay?"

She rolls her eyes at him. "No, we're both on our periods and need to hold each other to ease the pain."

His face pales as he rushes to the front of the store without another glance back.

"Okay, tell me everything, bitch."

And for the next twenty minutes, I do. In detail. It was hard to get most of it out amid her gasps and smart-ass comments. But I finally relay everything that's happened so far.

She grabs my shoulders and shakes them. "You've been holding out on me. I had no idea you were such a freak."

My cheeks blaze again. "I don't know what I'm doing. His voice… he makes me do shit I would never do with anyone else. But I'm starting to regret it. I think he might be a little weird."

She bursts into laughter. "You think? Was it when he made you lick up your own cum that gave you that impression? Or maybe when—"

"Oh my god, stop. I'm already ashamed as it is." I fold my arms to my chest and pace around our break room.

"Okay, maybe you didn't hear him right. You were super tipsy and in the throes of an orgasm. Or maybe someone did accidentally call you Roxy, and we just don't remember. What other explanation is there?"

I chew on my lower lip. "Yeah, maybe you're right. But I don't think I'm going to log on tonight. I need a break from whatever this is."

"Oh, shit!" Milo shouts.

Juniper hisses. "For fuck's sake, he can't watch the store for five fucking minutes without me."

I follow on her heels to find out what his problem is.

"What is it, Milo?" Juniper snaps.

"One of our regulars was robbed and murdered." He holds up his phone, showing us the news article.

I snatch it from him as soon as I see the picture of the guy. "What the fuck? He was literally just in here that same day." Barry was a little too chatty but always sweet and polite. I got the sense that he was working his way up to asking me out though.

Milo shakes his head as he takes his phone back. "No witnesses. Poor guy. It's weird that all they took was the cash from his wallet and his high school football ring."

My stomach knots. "What do you mean?"

Milo puts his phone back in his pocket. "Well, according to the article, he had another pile of cash lying on his bedside table. And a brand new lifted truck. Seems like a lot of trouble to kill someone over fifty bucks but not take anything else."

My blood goes cold. I usher Juniper into the back again. "Don't you think it's odd that this is the second person who's died after interacting with me?"

She shrugs. "Not really. There's no connection at all. It's shitty but not uncommon for that neighborhood."

I nod. Maybe she's right. I'm wound up so tight these days. Ever since the night at Joystick, I've been looking for some kind of release or escape. But I don't trust my own judgment.

"You're right. I'm being paranoid." I suck down the rest of my iced latte in one gulp.

"Let's go out and get fucked up tonight. It will take your mind off everything."

"That sounds perfect. I could use a few drinks. Thanks, babe."

"Should I tell RageMachine and Skat why we're not playing tonight? They might say something to Jack." She smirks at me with a mischievous gleam in her eye.

"Fuck it. I don't care. He can deal with not tormenting me for one night."

She laughs. "You mean tormenting your pussy."

I give her a playful shove. "Enough. See, this is why I didn't want to tell you."

As I walk back to my car, I think of Barry again. I can't believe someone murdered him hours after I talked to him. A chill snakes through me as I check my back seat before getting in. Nothing feels safe anymore.

CHAPTER 7

PUNK

MESSED UP. I GOT CARRIED AWAY AND CALLED HER ROXY BY MISTAKE. Fuck. Now she's not replying to any of my messages. But I'm not blocked so there's hope.

I glare at the headline on my phone. Looks like the police finally discovered my little temper tantrum. The article states they have no leads and no witnesses. Just another robbery gone bad on the wrong side of the tracks. Same shit, different day. It will never be traced back to me.

My heart races as I pace around my sunken living room. I pause to press my face against the cold glass. My floor-to-ceiling windows give me an unobstructed view of the Lavender Heights skyline. I can see the stars, the birds, and the monstrous skyscrapers. Normally it gives me a sense of peace. But tonight, I feel sick. Twisted. Desperate to hear my girl's voice again. Aching to see her in front of me on her knees.

I spent all day tailing her. She was at the record store for a short shift. Then a second latte at Pick Your Poison. Before heading home, she stopped at a department store, coming out with a few bags. I'm getting impatient.

I can only keep watching her for so long. The time is coming when I need to strike. To claim her. I've almost got her completely wrapped around my finger.

I log in to *After: 8113* and scour my friends list for Roxy's crew, praying they have an ongoing session open. It's ten p.m., and Roxy still hasn't joined the group chat. *I want to know why.*

I keep scrolling through my friends list and see RageMachine and Skat are online. I quickly send a request to join.

"What's up, guys," I say as nonchalantly as possible. "What's good?"

"Jackie boy. We're just chilling. You want to run the gauntlet quest with us? We could use a third," Skat asks.

"Yeah, for sure." My palms are sweating, mouth dry.

"Sweet. I'm tired of losing," RageMachine adds.

"Where are the girls tonight?" I ask casually.

"Out slutting it up or some shit," Skat snorts.

"They said they needed a girls' night." RageMachine snickers. "Which we all know is code for getting laid by some random dude in the backseat of a car."

An alert pops up from my phone. The tracker on Roxy's car is moving. What the fuck? She's driving toward downtown. My pulse kicks up a notch. But I take deep breaths, forcing myself to laugh with them. "Fucking women, right?"

They laugh and agree with me as we run and gun our way through the cavernous maze. But I keep one eye trained on the tracker. She's at Push. Fuck. Remembering what happened last time she went to a club makes my stomach turn. Why the fuck would she rather be out drinking than playing with me?

We make it to the end of the quest in record time. Rage and Skat shower me with a barrage of praises for helping them finally complete it.

"Anytime," I reply. "But I'm about to pass the fuck out now. Long day."

"For sure, for sure," Rage says.

We say our goodbyes and virtually high-five before I log off and power everything down. I grab my mask and throw my hood up over my head. It's time to go see what my girl is up to. I tuck my hunting knife into my combat boot, snatch the keys to my bike off the counter, and head out.

I ignore the looks from people as I stalk through the club wearing my glow-in-the-dark mask under my hood. Some of the women and men look intrigued, smirking at me with glazed eyes. Eye fucking me as if they have the right. The blade against my calf is practically begging to come out and play.

Strobe lights hit the dancefloor to the sounds of bass-heavy house music. The rest of the bar is lit up in pink and purple neon lights. It's a spectacle designed to seduce. To lower your inhibitions. A hunting ground for hungry deviants. But Roxy is off-limits. I just have to find her first.

I walk into another room and blink to adjust to the black lights. Swirls of filigree and ancient symbols dance across the walls—a cheap projector trick to invoke more lore and debauchery. The music is haunting in here, dark chords that drip feral.

My cock twitches when I see her. In a dark corner, wearing a short, black dress and sneaker pumps, Roxy sways her hips to the music. BratBaby—Juniper—is on the dancefloor, squished between two gym rats covered in body paint. I saddle up to one of them and pull him close.

"Keep this girl on the dance floor and away from her friend for the next hour. And I'll double it when I'm done." I slip a hundred-dollar bill into the sweaty man's hand.

He nods and goes back to dry humping Juniper's leg. Fucking hell. If these walls could only talk...

Flashbacks of all the fucked-up things I've done in here, back before I was sober, threaten to consume me. This place is wild. I've lost track of all the times I've snorted cocaine off that sleek obsidian bar. But there's only one drug I want tonight. I take a deep breath and stalk toward my pretty girl.

I nestle up behind her, pressing my chest to her back, and sway against her to the music. She starts to turn around, but I grab her hips and hold her in place. I hear her breath hitch.

"Jack and Jill went up the hill to fetch a pail of water..." I croon in her ear.

She freezes. "Fuck," she murmurs.

I press my masked face against her cheek. "Jack fell down and broke his crown, and Jill came tumbling after," I continue to whisper.

The bass thumps from the other room while the speakers in this room play a deep melodic melody fluttered by a cacophony of violins and piano keys. I snake my arm around her waist and pull her tighter to my chest.

A soft whimper escapes her lips. "Jack?"

My cock twitches. "Mmm, correct."

"What do you want from me?" she rasps.

I slide my other hand around her chest and grip her throat. "I want you to worship me on your knees."

She sucks in a sharp breath. "Oh god."

"I'm your fucking god now." I slide my hand down her waist and pull up the hem of her dress until I find the inside of her fleshy thigh. I grab onto it and squeeze. "I want you spread open... legs pressed back... hands tied... nipples swollen... while I devour your pussy like it's my last fucking meal on this earth."

Another whimper flutters out from between her full lips. She clenches her legs together, locking my hand in between them. "How did you find me, Jack?"

I inch my hand higher, forcing her to release her death grip on it. "No matter where you go, I'll find you, Roxy."

The lights dim again, casting us into a deeper level of darkness. The music changes; electronic synthesizers take hold of the speakers. A strobe light flashes over us, pulsing as hard as the ache in my cock.

She's so soft. So fucking pliable. I walk forward, nudging her farther into the corner until she's facing the wall. "*You're mine now.*"

I chuckle as she arches her back against me. I lift my hand again, inching her dress up even more until it's barely covering her ass. I'm blocking her from the crowd, and it's so fucking dark in here that this show is only for me.

"Jack... you can't do this. I don't know you. Please," she pleads.

"Shhh. Put your hands on the wall." I lean into her until her breasts crush against it.

She shudders when I find the edge of her panties and pull them to the side. "You're shaking, pretty girl."

"Y-yeah, because you're scaring me," she stammers.

I roll my thumb over her engorged clit, and my cock springs to life. I want my lips puckered around it. *Fuck.* I breathe heavily into her ear. "I think you're shaking because your pussy is in fucking heat."

She shakes her head. "You're a psycho. How long have you been stalking me?"

I press more of my body weight against her as I finger the outer lips of her sopping-wet pussy. She can protest all she wants, but I can *feel* how fucking bad she wants me. "*Brush off that dirt, for you're not hurt… Come up the hill with me, Jill… Let's fetch that pail of water.*"

"No. Let me go, Jack. Or whatever your real fucking name is." The way she squirms does something feral to me.

"Relax, Roxy. Fight all you want, but I'm not letting you get away." I plunge two fingers inside her pussy, push all the way in, and still myself there. I remove my other hand from her throat and shove those two fingers inside her mouth. I press down on her tongue, forcing her head back against me.

Her hips jerk back as she slams her palms against the wall. "Fuck," she whines. It's barely intelligible with my fingers in her mouth.

I add a third finger to her pussy and thrust back and forth. "You haven't returned any of my messages. I don't like being ignored, Roxy."

"I'm sorry," she mumbles through a whimper.

But I don't believe her. She's just upset she got caught. I take my fingers out of her mouth and grab a fist full of her silky dark hair and yank her head back so she's looking up at my masked face. "You're *my* girl, Roxy. *My slut.* Don't you ever fucking forget it. Tell me you're sorry again, but this time, I want you to mean it."

She's trembling again. I roll my thumb in circles around her clit, obsessed with how swollen it is for me. I can feel her fucking pulse inside it, beating faster than the music.

She cries against the wall. "I'm really sorry, Jack. So fucking sorry."

Mmm. Better. She's learning. Her juices leak down my wrist. "Good. Do you want to cum, pretty girl?"

Roxy's legs vibrate against mine. The projector goes black and then switches to flickering candlelight against the walls. It skates across her face, illuminating the chaotic hunger in her eyes. It's as if I can see her internally fighting with herself.

I press her head against the wall and growl in her ear. "Surrender to your god, Roxy."

She whimpers and releases a shaky breath. "What have you done to me?"

I smile beneath the mask as I scissor the folds of her pussy with my fingers. "I'm just getting started."

Her hips jerk forward and back as she slowly starts to grind against my hand. Thatta girl. "There she is. My perfect little slut." I tighten my grip on her hair as I drag my fingers back and up her ass crack.

She tries to shake her head. "No. Stop. I can't do this." She resists even as her essence soaks her thighs.

I sigh as I draw circles gently around her anus. "Shhh." I pull her dress all the way up around her waist. "Has anyone been back here before?" I wedge the tip of my finger inside her hole.

She gasps and clenches around me. "*No one.*"

My erection grows. Fuck. "Oh, that's very good. It saves me from having to kill another man for you."

"You're crazy," she whisper yells.

I find it amusing that in this room full of people, she hasn't even thought about screaming for help. That tells me all I need to know about my pretty girl. I know exactly what she wants. *What she needs.*

I remove my finger and slide it back down around to her clit again. "We'll save that one for another day." I thrust inside her again, rougher this time. I want her release on my fingers.

Her hips begin to rock again to a flurry of moans coming from her throat. "Damn you, Jack."

I chuckle as I release her hair. I caress her neck first, then her sweat-soaked chest. She's glistening like an angel. Like a holy ray of light that fights the devil at her back while stretching toward the darkness at the same time.

"Oh, fuck. Fuck you." She grunts and presses her forehead to the wall while she grinds against me.

I flick her clit with my thumb as I slide in and out of her cunt with three fingers. She's so slick. So needy. "I love how you submit to me," I growl in her ear.

A burst of liquid soaks my hand as she shudders against the wall. "Fuck… Oh shit. God. Fuck."

I flip her around to face me and pin her to the wall. "Don't ever ignore me again, Roxy. I know where you work. Where you live. *Everything* about you. You can't run *or* hide because I'll catch you before your feet even hit the ground."

She fixates on my eyes, trying to see beyond the x's that cover them through the mask. "Tell me your real name. I think it's only fair."

I tilt my head. "Not tonight. You've broken my trust, Jilly. You'll need to earn it back."

She bites her lip, and a blaze of fury flashes in her eyes. "Listen to me. Stay away from me. Don't message me. Stop following me. Leave me alone. Or I'll go to the police."

Oh, how I do wish she could see the smile behind my mask. "And tell them what? I have every single thing that you and I have done recorded. Do you really think they're going to believe you? Nah. Not with the record you have."

Her eyes widen. "How do you—"

I put my finger to her lips. "Yeah, I know all about your past. The sooner you accept that you're mine, the better. Just think of all the ways I'm going to make you cum, pretty girl."

Her throat bobs as she swallows back her fear. "Did you kill Barry?"

Ah, so that was his name. Bryce, Barry, same douche effect. "See, I think you're starting to get it. Now... grab your friend and go home, Roxy. It's late, and there are too many predators in here who would love to do vile things to you. But your pussy belongs to me. Unless murder turns you on. I'd be happy to slaughter a few more for you."

Her lip trembles, but she keeps her chin up, even though her juices continue to streak her legs. "N-No. Okay, Jack. I'll go home."

I caress her cheek with the back of my hand. "Thatta girl. Talk to you soon, Jilly."

CHAPTER 8

ROXY

PULL MY WET HAIR OUT FROM UNDER MY BATHROBE. I SHUDDER AS Juniper hands me a steaming cup of herbal tea. "There's something wrong with me," I murmur.

She flops down on the floor next to me and leans back against my couch. "How is any of this your fault?"

The memory of Jack's hand on my thigh, his fingers expertly stroking my pussy, makes my clit throb. "I liked it. The way he touched me, the dirty things he said to me… I fucking *loved* it."

She sighs. "Tell me again what happened."

I close my eyes and take myself back to earlier. "He came up behind me and pushed me up against the wall. He said that he would never let me get away. It scared me, but it also turned me on. I'm sick, aren't I? Fucking Stockholm syndrome or some shit."

She bites her lip to hide a smirk. "Relax. I bet it's just another game. There's nothing wrong with you. Maybe him. But definitely not you. Did you see his face?"

I shake my head. "No," I whisper. "He was wearing a mask… the same mask from our video chat."

"That's actually kind of hot. Sorry. But holy shit. It's like he walked straight out of one of our favorite dark romance novels." She lights up a joint, takes a puff, and hands it to me.

My cheeks heat. I take a long drag off the joint as I nod my head. "Right? Except this is real life, Juniper. He said he killed Barry. Hot or not, that's fucked up."

Juniper shrugs. "Meh. I mean who the fuck cares about Barry? Just go with it. He has a sexy voice and judging by the way you keep blushing, it sounds like he made you cum pretty fucking hard."

I pinch my eyes shut and massage my temples. "Fuck. I have to block him. He's dangerous."

She lifts an eyebrow. "And you aren't?"

A wave of nausea pulls at my belly. Juniper is the only one on this planet I've told my past to. "That was different."

"Maybe it's not. Jack may have had very valid reasons for kill-ing Barry. Maybe he found out that Barry had creepy intentions to-ward you. Maybe—"

"Oh fuck!" I gasp. "What if Jack was at Joystick that night? That guy jumped to his death after leaving a written confession to assault-ing me. You didn't see that guy. I don't believe for one second that he jumped. Maybe Jack was there, and he pushed him."

Her eyes widen. "Fuck. That's where his obsession with you started. It has to be. But if that's the case, well, Roxy, he did you a favor. That guy got what he deserved in my opinion."

I nod as another shudder rolls through me. "I was happy when I read that he was dead."

She scoots over to me and drapes her arm across my shoulders. "Same. Listen, I'm going to do something really best friend worthy for you. I'll talk to Milo and Coast and ask if they remember anything strange about that night. Maybe they saw something."

I chuckle. "Damn. Now I know you love me if you're willing to endure a conversation with those two when you don't have to."

She rubs my arm. "Of course I love you, bitch. As far as Jack goes, maybe stay away from the game for a couple of days. If he gets crazy, block the fucker."

Somehow I think that will only make it worse. "He knows where I work. He knew that I'd be at Push tonight. *He says he knows where I live.*"

We both glance at my front door at the same time.

"Do you want to sleep at my place tonight?"

I wince. "Thanks, but I caught your brother sniffing my underwear last time."

She bursts out laughing. "He was shitfaced and forgot where he was. Trust me, he's obsessed with some college chick."

"I'll take my chances here. Seriously though, I'll be fine. I bet Jack found out where we were from Rage and Skat. He's probably just trying to freak me out for his own amusement."

Juniper bounces up. "Exactly. And at least you got to cum on something other than your vibrator for a change."

I playfully punch her in the leg. "Hilarious. You should have your own stand-up comedy show."

We embrace, and I walk her to the door, making sure to keep watch until I see she's safely in her car. Once I'm alone again, a barrage of chills find their way up my spine and to the back of my neck.

Out of curiosity, I power on my console but leave my status set to offline. My stomach drops into my feet. Fuck. I have seven messages from Jack. I don't dare open them because he'll know I've read them. Instead, I shut it down and crawl under the covers of my memory foam bed.

It takes me hours to fall asleep. My heart is racing, my adrenaline pumping, and every little noise makes me flinch. His voice replays over and over again in my head: *you can't run or hide because I'll catch you before your feet even hit the ground.*

The sound of my alarm sends me flailing. Fuck, I don't remember it being this loud. I must've been in a really deep sleep. I turn all three of them off on my phone and roll over. I don't have to work today so I can squeeze in another hour or so. Last night drained me in more ways than one.

But I can't relax. Every time I close my eyes, I feel his hands on me. I hear his voice in my ear, his breath on my neck and my cheek. My juices leak into my panties. Fuck. A warm flush dances across my skin as the ache in my pussy grows. I haven't cum that hard… *ever.*

My ex, Aaron, would pump inside me a few times before convulsing his load onto my stomach. He never cared if I came or not. He never asked, assuming I was as satisfied as him. I mean, who wouldn't be after getting repeatedly stabbed in the cunt with an average-size dick for three minutes? I roll my eyes at the ceiling, annoyed by the memory.

I force myself out of bed and drag my feet to the kitchen. It takes the aroma of coffee brewing to bring my eyes from half-slits to wide open, but it's that first delicious sip that brings me back to life.

With the sunlight streaming in from my bay window, last night's events seem less dangerous. I had too much to drink and overreacted. Yes, it's odd that he knew where I was. But like Juniper said, Skat and Rage probably let it slip. You can't trust boys to keep their mouths shut. They gossip more than my Aunt Myrtle's book club after church every Sunday.

What *does* still feel fresh is the way he touched me. The sensations that he drew out of me. It was like one of my wildest fantasies brought to life. I've never met a man like Jack before. He's demanding and controlling, but he also wants to make me cum until I can't see straight. This new feeling of being sexually satisfied is one I could get used to. I'm just not entirely sure I'm willing to pay the price. How far is Jack going to push me?

I shudder and immediately put on another pot of coffee, seeing as the first one is almost gone already. I refill my mug, which looks more like a bowl with a handle, and plop down on my couch. I pull my pink fuzzy blanket over my lap and count to ten. I have to look at his messages. *I want to.* His forwardness scares me a little, but I can't help but get sucked back in.

My fingers tremble around the controller as I click on the first message.

You tasted so good on my fingers I had to lick them clean.

Oh fuck. My breath hitches. Why the fuck is that so hot? The temperature in my body rises as I move to the second message.

Does your pussy miss me? Play with her for me until we meet again.

I squirm against the cushions. A flurry of goosebumps commands the skin on my arms. Holy hell. This man is sinful and saintly at the same time. But a twinge of uneasiness stirs in my gut. *Until we meet again.* He assumes that we will. That's a bit alarming.

The next three messages only get hotter and more depraved.

You're going to look so pretty trying to swallow my cock. I'll lick the tears from your cheeks.

And then I'll tie you up… blindfold you… and watch you squirm in the dark. Until you're screaming my name, begging for the slightest touch. You'll be so starved for it that you'll cum from just the brush of my lips on your neck.

I'm going to take care of you, pretty girl. I'll scrub off the filth of everyone who's ever touched you. You're mine now, Roxy.

I gasp and almost drop the controller. Fuck. I pull the blanket up to my neck, shivering as I read the filthy things he wants to do to me. If this were a romance novel, I'd be so jealous of the main character. But this is real life. *My* life. And fantasies exist for a reason. They don't make logical sense outside our heads.

I blow out a deep breath and click on the second to last message.

I have a present for you, pretty girl. Something to help loosen you up.

Fucking hell. My palms sweat. Last message.

Check your front door.

I freeze. A wave of nausea starts in the pit of my stomach and inches up my throat, threatening my equilibrium. I pinch my eyes shut and count to ten. *Surely he's just fucking with me, right?*

I push myself up from the couch and stagger to my door. With each step, the trembles in my body increase. I look out the peephole first to double-check that there's not a masked man standing on my porch. My fingers shake as I unlatch the chain, then the deadbolt, and finally turn the bottom lock, then the knob.

My eyes dart to the street, glancing around to see if I can spot anyone unusual. But my neighborhood is quiet as it always is on Sunday mornings. I look down to see a small pink heart-shaped box with a bow on top. I swear to god, this better not be someone's finger. But that would be absurd. I really need to stop watching true crime shows by myself.

I snatch the box, dash back inside, and relatch all the locks. I pant against the door, holding the box out in front of me like it's a bomb. Oh shit. What if it is a fucking bomb? He said he wanted to loosen me up. Maybe he meant because my body parts would be splattered all over my apartment. Fuck. *Breathe, Roxy. Just breathe.*

And yet I still hold it an arm's length away from me as I walk to the kitchen table and set it down. I take another deep breath and lift the lid off. Oh god. Another wave of nausea hits me. It's a fucking anal plug. *And a tube of lubricant.*

There's also a note that reads: *Get nice and wet before you put this in, pretty girl. And don't take it out. I'll remove it myself next time I see you.*

My knees wobble as I read his words a few more times. My brain isn't processing. This man *does* know where I fucking live. He was right outside while I slept. Fuck. I have a fucking stalker. When I begged the universe to send me someone who's obsessed with me, I didn't mean fucking literally.

A rush of adrenaline shoots through my veins as I dash over to the couch and pick up my controller. I click on his profile and hover the cursor over the block button. My breaths are coming in quick short bursts. My heart is racing. If I do this, it could anger him. I don't know what he's capable of, but I feel in my gut that he's dangerous.

And yet he's the one I dream about. The first person I think about when I wake up and the last person before I go to sleep. I picture his mask when I'm fucking my vibrator. I hear his voice in my head every time I cum.

I should block him and go to the police. But I don't trust *them* either. They didn't believe me back then. Instead, they threw me into juvie until I was eighteen. Attempted murder without probable cause. Fucking bullshit. It was self-defense. My momma knew it. That monster of a husband of hers knew it when I drove the knife into his gut. But it didn't matter. He was the police chief's son. And I was the daughter of an incarcerated drug dealer.

I spent two years in there. Two years because I had the audacity to try and kill the man who abused me every day. Those records are supposed to be sealed. But Jack, or whatever the fuck his name is, knows about it. That intrigues me more than it scares me.

I thought I'd left my past behind. I moved here to Lavender Heights to go to school. To start fresh. It was a miracle I got that dance scholarship. Only to lose it ten months later after the fall. I've been withdrawn and apathetic ever since. But it's been three years. And Jack has awakened something in me that I thought had died. He's lit my fire again.

A chill snakes up my spine. I swallow down the lump in my throat as I dig deep for my courage. I pick up the controller and reply to his last message.

Don't come near my house again. Or I'll stab you like I did him.

I hit send, wait for him to read it, and then block his profile. Let's see what happens when Jack actually comes tumbling down.

CHAPTER 9

PUNK

I CHUCKLE WHEN I READ HER REPLY. I TAKE IT SHE FOUND THE BOX I left her. I start to respond when the chat disappears. My stomach knots. I click on my friends list and scroll. I can't find her. I type her gamertag into the search bar. No results. No JillChick22. Fuck. She fucking blocked me.

Oh, Roxy. I think it's time you meet the real me.

The sky is bright orange when I pull up to Vinyl Delights. It casts a glow that makes the ground look like it's on fire. I park my bike in front and peer through the window. Roxy laughs with Juniper behind the counter. She looks stunning when she smiles. Her whole face lights up like tonight's sunset.

I remove my helmet and walk in, avoiding eye contact as I head straight toward the classic grunge section. Within minutes Juniper calls out, "Holler if you need anything."

I pause my browsing and turn my head to the side, giving them my profile. "I'll let you know."

They continue chatting, but I can feel both of their eyes on me. They're curious. I look familiar. I may even sound familiar. She'll wonder where she's heard my voice before. And when I turn around to face them, she'll recognize me from TV. Her brain will convince her that's how she knows my voice.

I smirk with my back turned as I peruse the vinyl stacks. When I finally find the one I'm looking for, I put it under my arm and stalk toward the counter. Their eyes widen as I approach. Roxy licks her lips, drinking in the sight of me. All six foot three inches of me. In my leather jacket, faded band tee, and ripped jeans, I'm very aware of the effect I have on women. I'm almost angry that she's checking me out since she doesn't even know yet that Punk and Jack are one and the same. Should I be jealous of myself?

When I place Nirvana's *In Utero* album on the counter, their mouths drop open. Five. Four. Three. Two. O—.

"Oh my god. You're Punk Wilder," Juniper blurts out with zero decorum.

I run a hand through my dirty-blond hair, fingering the waves back off my forehead. I glance back and forth between them in an attempt to look nervous about being spotted. "Um… yeah. You know me?"

She snort laughs. "*Everyone* knows you, dude."

I dip my head, feigning shyness. "For sure. You skate?"

"Yeah, right. Roxy used to though."

Roxy's face turns bright red. It's adorable. "Oh, yeah? You get up to Heights Park lately? I just helped them build a new ramp."

She folds her arms over her chest, defensively. "My friend here is embellishing as *usual.* I haven't touched a skateboard since I was twelve."

I tilt my head and relish how the blush of her cheeks inches down her chest, consuming her. I bet her nipples are two stiff peaks under that fuzzy sweater. The corners of my lips turn up into a smirk. "And what about skateboarders?"

Juniper stifles a laugh.

Roxy narrows her eyes at me. "Have we met before?"

"I get that a lot." I don't take my eyes off her. Deep inside, she knows me. Her mind will rationalize a thousand different things. But Roxy Luna knows my voice better than anyone. She's the only one I talk to the way I do.

"I bet you do," Juniper drawls.

I keep my gaze fixed on Roxy as she rings me up for the record. "You a gamer chick, Roxy?"

Her breath hitches, and her fingers freeze around the record. "Why would you think that?" she snaps.

I hold up my hands in mock defense. "So you hate video games. Noted. I was just wondering if you've played my game. Since you used to skate, I figured you could check it out."

She blows out a deep breath while her friend stalks off, shaking her head. "Sorry. Um, yeah. I am a gamer. But I don't play sports games."

I can't tell if she's confused, angry, aroused, or all three. But I'm enjoying every second of flustering her. "Fair enough."

She drops the receipt in the bag before handing it to me. "This is a great album by the way. One of my favorites from that era."

Our hands lightly brush in the exchange, and it sends a shiver of excitement directly to my cock. "Same. I collect copies of it wherever I go. It got me through some tough times."

For the first time since she laid eyes on me, her expression soft-ens. My story is not a secret. I led a very public downward spiral for all the world to see.

"What's your favorite song on it?" she asks, biting her lip.

My fingers tingle. I want to reach over and touch her so fuck-ing bad. "Heart-Shaped Box."

We stare at each other for what seems like an eternity, locked in the grip of the chemistry between us. She finally draws in breath. A storm rages in her eyes. She takes a step back. "I better get back to work. Nice meeting you in person, Punk."

I wink. "Likewise, Roxy."

I tuck the record inside my leather jacket and zip it up before hopping back on my bike. I glance back through the store window before putting my helmet on. Sure enough, she's still staring after me. She's a clever girl, as smart as she is beautiful. It won't be long until she figures out who's come to claim her. Soon, she'll be kneeling in front of me with her tongue out, as addicted to me as I am to her.

I lean against my bike, devouring my sandwich as I watch Oliver try to teach the new kid how to do a kickflip over a trash can. He's agile and fearless in every attempt. No matter how many times he eats shit. They've asked me countless times to help instruct, but I don't have the stomach for it anymore. It hurts too much, knowing that I can never skate like I used to. It's a miracle they even asked, con-sidering the size of the match I used to burn my whole fucking life down. I guess time helps people forget. Or at least soften the blow.

But I still like to come out here and watch. It quiets the rage for a little while. And it makes these kids want to push themselves hard when they see their idol standing by on the sidelines. I cause a stir every time I show up. At least I gave them an example of what *not* to do when you get a bunch of money and fame. Skaters have always had an edge to them. A mystique. But I took bad boy to a whole other level. I became the villain.

The old-school cats still show me respect, but the people who really matter—the sponsors, my family, my fucking friends… They gave up on me a long time ago. Getting clean didn't matter. I lost their trust. I don't fucking blame them for turning their backs. I did some really horrible shit.

But now I have Roxy. And I'm going to make sure she never wants to leave me. She's an outcast like me, broken, lonely, and misunderstood. When I found out that she also lost her career over an injury I felt even closer to her. We are cut from the same cloth. We are destiny.

I look down at my phone and check the tracker I have on her car. It's moving toward her apartment. I throw my sandwich wrapper in the trash, wave to Oliver, and fire up my bike. As I drive over to her neighborhood, I contemplate my next move.

Part of me wants to knock on her door and demand that she unblock me. But I'm not ready to show my cards just yet. I need to know that she wants me too. And not because I'm Punk Wilder but because I'm the man who made her cum harder than she ever has.

It doesn't take a genius to figure that out. The second I slid my fingers inside her wet cunt, when I felt her folds tremble against me, I knew she hadn't been touched like that before. It made me hungrier, needier, for her release. The way she fucking shuddered when she shattered all over my hand… Fuck. I became addicted to that sensation right then and there. Now I want to see what else I can elicit from her. What I can provoke out of her.

I kill the engine and park a block away from her apartment, leaving my helmet on just in case. She hops out of her car and darts up the stairs with a fury. Like she's late for something. Interesting. I nod at the old lady walking her dog. She eyes me cautiously, so I take off my helmet and hold up a random map on my phone.

"I think I'm lost. You know how to get back to the main road?"

She keeps her distance but relaxes a little. "Turn around and head straight for three blocks, then take a right. You'll run right into downtown."

I nod. "Thank you, ma'am. Have a good night."

She hurries off, not bothering to look back. I take my time putting my helmet on and revving my engine. As soon as she turns onto another street, I drive closer to Roxy's place. Her lights are on, and I can see her shadow darting around. It's not her usual behavior when she's settling in for the night.

"What are you up to, pretty girl?" I mumble to myself. The need to touch her again is festering, consuming my every waking thought and even my dreams. That is when I'm able to actually fall asleep.

Another thirty minutes tick by when I see her front door fly open. It's pitch black out now with few streetlights. She doesn't spot me as she barrels down the stairs and jumps into her car. Looks like my little doll is going out. I guess that means I am too.

I hang back for fifteen minutes before driving to where the tracker is headed. Back to Push. I smirk. *Someone hoping they have another run-in with their favorite masked man?*

By the time I arrive, there's already a line forming around the block. I take off my helmet and walk right past it to the front entrance. No mask tonight. Just me. The bouncer gives me a nod and steps aside. I've spent so much fucking money in here over the years, I'm surprised they haven't changed the name from Push to Punk.

The crowd parts as I walk through the strobe-lit club. Let the whispers and eye fucking commence. I can't keep the smirk from forming on my lips. I forget how good this feels sometimes. The power of commanding a room with just my presence. I can bend and break anything and anyone.

I spot Roxy at the main bar. Her hair is piled up in a messy bun, revealing a snake tattoo on the back of her neck. Fucking hell. I want to drag my tongue in circles around it until her knees give out. She looks like my own personal feast in tight jeans, a black lace bustier, and red heels. Well, that's a surprise. She's never been out in anything other than sneaker wedges. Is she wearing those sexy stilettos for me?

I saunter up to the bar a few feet from her and her friends, giving enough space for them to think I haven't seen them. I nod to the bartender, who I used to buy coke from, and he comes right over.

"What's good, Punk? You still clean?" He wipes a spot in front of me with a wet rag.

I nod. "Yup. I'll take a cranberry and soda."

He snickers. "That's a shame. I just got a new batch. Shit will make you orgasm."

If he doesn't shut the fuck up soon, I'm going to add him to my list of murder victims. I give him a wink. "My cock orgasms just fine, thanks."

I take the mocktail from him and turn toward Roxy while still pretending not to notice her. Out of the corner of my eye, I see them staring. My belly does a little flip. I wish it weren't so loud in here so I could hear what they're saying. Although, I imagine it's of the should we or shouldn't we variety.

What are the odds that I bought a record from them earlier and then showed up at their favorite club on the same day? Zero. Just me and my obsession with this exquisite creature. When she realizes all I've done to get next to her, she'll stop fighting it and submit. I'm so fucking close.

And they're on the move, inching toward me. My adrenaline spikes, sending little tremors down my shaft. My eyes widen, feigning surprise when they approach.

"Twice in one day," I drawl. "You aren't stalking me, are you?" I almost make myself laugh out loud.

Roxy blushes. "I come here all the time. What's your excuse?"

Sweat beads in between her breasts, which are pushed up by the bustier like a shelf I want to rest my face on. The way I'd twirl the tip of my tongue around each one of her nipples…

"I used to come here a lot back in the day. When I was a raging alcoholic and drug addict. Sometimes I pop in now just for nostalgia." Not entirely a lie.

Her expression softens and a flicker of sadness flashes through her eyes. Not pity. Empathy. Another reason why I love this girl.

"You're not tempted?" Juniper shouts over the music even though I can hear her just fine.

I narrow my eyes at her. "Every day. That's why it's called an addiction."

She winces. "Sorry."

That was too harsh. *Fuck.* I smile and touch her arm. "No worries. You didn't offend me."

Roxy studies me. Her throat bobs, quickening her breath as she takes in every detail about me. I know the signs because it's what I've done to her countless times.

"I still feel like we've met before." Roxy crosses her legs and locks her ankles. She's already clenching that pussy.

I shift closer to her and rest my arm against the bar. "Maybe we knew each other in a past life."

Her eyes light up as she grins. "What, like fated mates or something?"

I scoot closer. Now I can feel her body heat radiating. "Something like that. You never know."

I take another step so she has to crane her neck to look up at me. Her thick lips glisten, salivating for more of me. Her eyes glaze with lust and drunkenness.

"Not sure if I believe in all that." Roxy drops her gaze to my tattooed hands. She runs her finger over the black heart on my thumb. "Are you a hopeless romantic, Punk?"

Her touch sends an electric shock through my system. I have to use all my willpower to keep from pushing her back into that dark corner again. "Not hopeless."

I lick my lips and glance down at the button of her jeans and then back up. "You're really pretty, you know."

Her body stiffens, and she takes a step back. "Don't say that."

My curiosity piques. "Why not?"

She bites her lower lip as she plays with the straw in her drink, swishing it around in circles. "It's complicated. You're like super-hot, and I already feel like I know you but… I have a situationship that I'm dealing with."

I can't keep the grin off my face. She's trying to reject me because of her feelings for *me*. Well, a different me, but it's hilarious all the same. I hold back my laughter. "I can respect that. He's a lucky man, Roxy."

She pinches her eyes shut and swallows hard before gazing back up at me. "You say my name like he does."

Is she figuring it out? Impossible. There's no way in hell she's going to put this together. To her, the man standing before her is a celebrity she has a crush on, a man who she just happened to bump into. Twice.

But I can't help myself. I lean in until my lips brush her ear. "Do you like the way it sounds in my mouth?"

Her breath hitches, and she grips the edge of the bar. "Y-yes," she stammers. "It reminds me of him."

I draw in a deep breath, savoring her peaches and cream scent. "Understood. It was nice to see you again… Roxy."

I set my glass down on the bar and walk away, leaving her flushed and breathless. I'm so pleased with myself I could float on this new high. Because this kind doesn't end up with me face down in a dirty toilet. This new addiction isn't going to leave track marks on my arms. But I do hope she does leave scars on my body. I want her marks all over me so I can tattoo them there permanently.

The crisp air feels better than usual tonight. I ride through the back streets first and then make my way over to the ocean. The wind chops up the waves so hard I can feel the spray all the way from the road that runs along its rocky cliffs. I lick the salt off my lips with a smile. I wonder which persona of mine she'll fantasize about tonight when she's thrusting her vibrator in and out of her slick cunt. Maybe both.

By the time I get back to my penthouse, it's almost two in the morning. But I'm wide awake, energized from the brief encounter with Roxy.

"Let's see if anyone's still up playing," I mutter.

I turn on my console and headset and lean back against my

leather sofa. My chat requests are numerous, as usual. I change my status to offline as I scroll through them or else I'll get inundated with game invites.

My pulse quickens when I reach the bottom of the list. I lean forward and blink my eyes a few times. It's a new message from JillChick22. *She unblocked me.* My fingers tingle as I click on her chat icon.

Pre cum oozes from the tip of my cock when I read her words. Holy fuck.

I'm "wearing" your gift, and I'm ready to play.

CHAPTER 10

ROXY

EVERYTHING THROBS. MY HEART, MY HEAD, MY PUSSY. EVERY. Thing. There are too many signs and coincidences. It's like the universe keeps shoving me toward him. I need to keep going. My desire outweighs my fear.

Meeting Punk Wilder was not on my bingo card today. Running into him twice was fate. I've watched all his interviews and skate footage tons of times. And I saw him from far away once… Maybe that's why he seemed so familiar to me.

He's a cultural icon even despite his fall from grace. In person, he's even more charismatic *and* hot as fuck. Something about him reminded me of Jack. Punk has the same cadence to his tone. The same raspiness. And he commands attention the way Jack does.

And so here I am, drunk as fuck, and waiting for Jack to see my message with that anal plug still wedged inside me. I had to coat it with lube three times before it slid in without hurting. The longer it was in, the more I stretched around it. By the time I left Push, the sensation was making my nipples hard and my pussy tingle.

At one point, I had to lock my legs together just to keep them from shaking. Fuck. I want to cum so fucking bad. And I want to hear Jack's voice when I do.

I've been sitting erect on the edge of my couch with my legs locked at the knee since I got home at one a.m. After taking off my jeans and bustier, I decided to put on the nipple clamps as well.

I pour myself another glass of wine and try not to think about the wetness in my panties. I remind myself that Jack is a murderer, a stalker, and a stranger whose face I've never seen. But it's not enough to keep my clit from spasming. There is something deeply wrong with me.

I jump when my screen pings, and a message alert pops up. I jerk forward to grab my controller, and the plug twists in my anus. "Ohhh. Shit." I still myself and wait for the fluttering in my pussy to pass. *I can't believe I'm edging myself.*

I take a deep breath and click on the message.

Let's play then, pretty girl.

Heat floods my body when the invite to voice chat follows. It takes everything I have to not grind against the couch. I turn on my headset and mic.

"Do you like my gift?" he asks.

My legs shake. "Yeah," I rasp.

He breathes heavily into his mic. "I want to see you. Turn on your cam."

I hesitate for a second, wondering if I should go grab my mask. Fuck. He already knows what I look like. Fuck it. I click it on to see his glow-in-the-dark mask staring back at me. He's wearing a black hoodie with a baseball cap underneath it.

"There she is," he murmurs. "You made me angry, Jilly girl. But look at you now… wet and ready for my commands."

Fucking hell. I'm addicted to this. To the way he degrades and humiliates me for his own twisted amusement. "I want to see your face."

He clicks his tongue. "Shhh. Not yet. Open your legs. I want to see you enjoy that stretch."

Oh fuck. Sweat streams down my body as I lean back and slowly pull my legs apart. The farther they spread, the deeper the plug burrows in. I let out a whimper.

"Mmm. You better get used to it, pretty girl. My cock is much bigger than that. And not as gentle."

A flutter of tingles spread through my core. "Please, Jack. Take off your mask."

He shakes his head. "Not until I give you your punishment for blocking me."

For fuck's sake. I'm going to explode. I'm so close to the edge. "Fine. What do you want me to do?"

He chuckles. "First, I want you to take off your panties and stuff them in your mouth."

My stomach drops. Holy fuck. I've never done anything like this before. He makes me do these things, and I let him. I slide my panties down and off. As I bring them toward my mouth, I can smell my own arousal. Fuck. He sits quietly, waiting, *expecting* me to obey. And I do.

A deep moan escapes me as I taste myself.

"Yeah. That's my naughty little slut. Suck those panties clean.

You like the taste, don't you?" He leans forward as if he's trying to get a closer look. "Mmm. I know you do."

My head buzzes from the alcohol, making me dizzy. I lean forward to stop the spinning.

"Now I want you to reach down between your legs. Can you do that for me? Slide the plug out halfway and then push it back in deeper. As far as you can get it."

I'm practically hyperventilating. My pussy aches, my nipples are swollen, and my jaw is tingling from the salivation. As I pull the plug slowly out, my toes curl. I bite back a moan as the ribbed edges rub against my tender entrance.

"Hold on, pretty girl. Turn around so I can watch."

Fucking hell. I can barely breathe as I flip around. On my knees, I brace one hand on the top of my couch while I continue. There's something so hot about him watching me obey him.

"I can't wait to wrap my lips around that now that it's been inside you. Good girl. Now push it all the way in for me. Let me see how you stretch."

I bite down hard on my tongue through my black lace thong, drawing blood. The plug makes me feel so full, I can't imagine what his cock could do. I shudder as little pricks of electricity skate across the backs of my thighs. What the fuck? Oh, god. *It's vibrating*.

I white-knuckle the back of the couch as I moan around my panties.

"Even from here, I control your pleasure, pretty girl. Mmm. I love seeing you submit," he admits.

I rub my pussy against the cushions while the plug buzzes deep inside me. I feel feral, wild, like a rabid fucking animal who needs to be put down. My hips are in mid-roll when he increases the intensity.

A deep growl unleashes from my throat. I slide up and down the fabric in a fury, desperate for my release.

"Shhh, relax, baby. You're getting too worked up." He turns off the vibration to the plug. "Take deep breaths and calm down."

I spit my panties out as a flash of rage sparks through me. *I need to cum*. "You've done this to me," I pant. "*You* got me worked up."

He chuckles. "You did this, Roxy. You sat around all night waiting for me with your ass stuffed. You're a wild thing that needs to be tamed. That needs to be broken in. It's a good thing I'm here now."

Is he right? He didn't tell me to put the nipple clamps on. I did that to myself. I'm so consumed with need and ache. I shake my head, annoyed with myself. No. He's manipulating me again. "Fuck you, Jack," I hiss.

I wrap my pink fuzzy blanket around me and spin back around. "Fuck. You."

He leans back. "You're mad. But you know I'm right. I'm the god you've been praying for. The one who's going to always bring you to your knees and make you cum harder than you ever have. I'm the one who will worship this sacred vow between us. What we are is smoke and fire. Stop trying to convince yourself that you don't want to get burned. I know you crave my control. So fucking *submit*."

No. I don't want to be this way. Why do I enjoy this so much? It's sick and twisted and filthy. And I refuse to submit to a faceless man.

"Not until you take off your mask," I grit out.

He lets out a deep sigh. "Not tonight, Roxy. You're not ready."

Ugh. I could fucking scream. I snicker back at him. "Take it off right now or else I'm blocking you for real. No takebacks. I will never play this game with you again."

He tilts his head to the side. "Don't be a brat."

I gasp. "How dare you? I have every right to know who you really are. You don't get to stalk me all over town and then expect me to just give in. I will not play with shadows."

He stares at the screen silently for what seems like forever while I sit here shivering. I'm running out of patience. The more time that passes, the less I believe he's going to give me what I want.

I sigh. "Goodbye, Jack." I turn off the camera and my headset before he can respond. And then I block him. Again.

I toss and turn, sweating under the blankets. My head pounds and my heart races as I fight the spins. I've been in and out of restless sleep for what feels like an eternity. A purgatory of exhaustion, anxiety, and inebriation. I try to convince myself that it was the half joint I smoked and not the six cocktails and bottle of wine I pounded. But it was both. Ugh. I'm never drinking again.

As I turn toward my nightstand to reach for my water, my ass throbs. Oh no. I reach in between my legs and find the anal plug still inside. Fuck. I can't believe I passed out before removing it.

I slide my panties off, spread my legs, and take a deep breath. Fuck, this is going to hurt.

"Don't you fucking dare," a voice rasps in the dark.

I freeze. Oh shit. Fuck. My breath hitches as my adrenaline

kicks up three levels. My heart races. He's here. *He's in my fucking house.*

Jack stalks toward my bed, tall with broad shoulders and energy so dominant he could force molecules to split.

He towers over me, his mask glowing. "I didn't give you permission to take that out yet."

"Please… don't murder me." My chest heaves as I fight to catch my breath, which feels impossible with my heart beating out of control.

He brushes a matted strand off my forehead with his gloved hand. "I'll take off the mask if you agree to submit. And I mean, for real this time, Roxy."

My endorphins spike, mixing my emotions into a toxic blender of fear, arousal, and curiosity. All I've wanted since this game began is to see his face. To see the man who can shatter me with just his voice. But what am I giving up? What the fuck will happen to me if I surrender?

He drags his leather fingers down my cheek, then my jaw. I gasp as he wraps his hand around my throat. "You're just as obsessed as I am. Quit prolonging the inevitable and submit. Then we can play for real."

I shudder as he controls my pulse, my heart rate, and the tingling in my traitorous fucking pussy. *Fucking Stockholm syndrome bullshit.* This is what I've fantasized about. Dreamed about. And now he's here, in the flesh, ready to break me to his will. But I'm more afraid that he'll leave if I say no.

"Okay, Jack." I put my hands above my head and whisper, "I submit."

He shivers as he releases a deep breath. "Good because I'm done playing with my food. I'm ready to eat."

Fucking hell. He's going to be the death of me. Hopefully not literally. He removes his gloves first. A familiar tattoo catches my eye. A black heart on his thumb. Did I see his hands in the video chat earlier? My memory is hazy under the weight of a long list of alcoholic regrets.

My belly flutters as he slowly unties the mask from his head. "There's no turning back now, pretty girl."

I gasp as he lets it drop to the floor, revealing his face. The face of *Punk fucking Wilder*. Holy hell. Now I remember the black heart tattoo on his hand. "I don't understand. Earlier, at the record store, and at the club… you tricked me. *You lied to me.*" I wonder if this would shock me less if I were sober. Or maybe it would just make me angrier.

He licks his lips. "I've never lied to you. You heard and saw what you wanted to." He leans over me and places his hands on either side of my head. "But your body knew what your mind couldn't figure out."

Every nerve ending on my skin feels stripped, raw, and delicate like a live wire. I ball my fists into the sheets, clenching the silky fabric to brace myself against the onslaught of sensory overload. "You've been stalking me since the party at Joystick." It's not a question. I know it in my bones.

He retreats back, taking a seat on the black velvet chair by the window, the one I usually drape my clothes on when I'm too lazy to hang them up. But I was so drunk earlier that they didn't make it past the floor.

He leans back and spreads his legs. "I noticed you the second you walked in. I watched you all night, wishing I was the straw you puckered your lips around. Craving every inch of you—your throaty laugh, wanting those devilish smirks reserved only for me… desperate to lick the peaches and cream off your skin."

My stomach knots while my clit spasms. My body is confused, terrified, and turned on. Fuck. "What else happened that night, Punk? What else did you see?"

He takes off his ballcap and runs his long, slender fingers through his dirty-blond strands. "I saw you bolt down the stairs toward the bathrooms. So I followed. I waited. I paced back and forth as more and more women came out. But not you. Women who had gone in after you came out. I knew something wasn't right."

The acrid taste of bile coats the back of my throat as I remember that creep's hands up my skirt. "The line was too long, so I went next door to the gas station," I murmur.

His hazel eyes darken, narrowing at me. "You shouldn't have left by yourself."

My hands tremble and ache as I bunch the bedsheets tighter. "I know."

"When I threw the back door open, you ran past me so fast… you were in shock. Scared. Distraught. And when I saw the look on that pig's face, I knew that he violated you… I knew you were mine and that I would brutally slaughter anyone who dares to touch you."

Shivers crawl up my spine while juices leak from my pussy. He murdered a man in cold blood for me. That death is on both of us. But it doesn't make me angry or terrified like it should. His behavior is erratic, possessive, and unhinged… and I like it.

"I never believed that he jumped to his death… Thank you."

He smirks. "That's what your god does for you, pretty girl. Now it's time for your holy sacrament."

My pulse kicks up another notch when he gets up and stalks back over to the bed. "Turn onto your stomach."

Trembling, I do as he says. I draw in a sharp breath when he skates his fingers up the back of my thighs. "What are you going to do to me?"

He runs his palms over my ass cheeks. "Well, first I'm going to take this plug out. You've been such a good girl holding it for me."

I whimper as his fingers probe my entrance.

"Shhh, relax." He grips the plug and slowly twists it in circles. "Mmm. Look at that stretch. You're almost ready for more."

Spasms burst in my core as he plays with the plug, rotating it from side to side while inching it in and out. "Please..."

He spreads my ass apart. I shiver as I feel the tip of his tongue lash between my cheeks. He grips the plug with his teeth and yanks it out.

A whimper escapes my throat. I miss the feel of it already. The way it rubbed against my tender flesh, stimulating every nerve.

Punk chuckles. "Don't be sad, pretty girl. Tomorrow, you're getting a new one. Every day you'll get a bigger one. I have to break you in first before you can handle my cock."

"*Fuck*," I whimper. My legs shake uncontrollably against the mattress.

He goes back to the chair and sits down. "I brought over some ice cream. I want you to go get it for me."

I roll over before sitting up. I brace my hands on the side of the bed, my head dizzy. The devious look in his eyes lets me know this is part of the game. The submission.

I start to stand up and he shakes his head. "On your knees,

Roxy. You will crawl to the kitchen, get me a bowl of ice cream, and crawl back. Go. *Fetch.*"

He gets off on humiliating me. And I let him because a sick part of me likes it too. I like the way his gaze hungers for me when I lower myself to the floor. In just a tight white tank top, my ass bare, I crawl across my own bedroom while he sits and watches in silence.

When I get to the kitchen, I stand up just to get the pint of vanilla ice cream out of the freezer, scoop some into a bowl, and grab a spoon. *Fuck.* I press my forehead against the cold stainless steel of the fridge. *How the hell am I going to crawl back with this?*

CHAPTER 11

PUNK

THE SIGHT OF MY PRETTY GIRL INCHING ALONG THE FLOOR ON her knees stirs something so primal in me I can hardly sit still. She takes her time, balancing on one hand while she pulls herself forward. Every time the metal spoon clanks against the bowl, a tingling pulse sparks down my swollen shaft.

"If you spill even a drop, I'll make you lick it up," I growl.

She stops halfway to readjust her grip. "I won't."

The way she cares for that bowl amuses me. It's all I can do to keep from knocking it out of her hand just so I can watch her lap it up. To see her pretty pink tongue leave wet spots on the plush carpet.

Her eyes light up as she nears me, grateful that her degradation is almost over. But little does she know, it's only beginning.

"Wait." I put my hand up. "Take your shirt off. And don't you dare set that bowl down on the floor."

She sighs and starts to rise, but I put my hand up again.

"I did not give you permission to sit up."

"What the fuck? How am I… I can't," she whines.

I chuckle while I watch her struggle.

She turns her head in. Using her teeth she pulls down the string of her tank, inching it over her shoulder. Then she turns and does the same to the other one. I lean forward, mesmerized.

"Thatta girl. Not just a pretty face. So very clever."

She draws her arms in. As she tugs the string farther down with her teeth she has to contort her body, lowering herself until her belly is flush against the carpet. My cock throbs as I watch her get the strap over her wrist and pull her hand out. She does the same on the other side, passing the bowl to the free hand.

I'm beyond impressed and fucking feral for this creature. She's so eager to please me. So desperate for my approval. "You *are* ravenous to pray at my altar, aren't you?"

She glares back at me, but behind the anger is a desire so dark, so deep, it could start a fire. This entire room would go up in flames.

She huffs again and inches forward on her belly, wiggling from side to side. The closer she gets, the farther her tank top slides down. By the time she reaches my feet, it's around her calves.

I thread my fingers through her dark strands as I yank her head up. "You're going to regret taking so long," I rasp with a smirk. I yank the bowl out of her hands and set it on the small reading table next to me.

Her skin is flushed, bright-red with carpet burns. "But I didn't spill any."

Fuck, this woman is so perfect. So fucking sexy it's almost vile. "Come, sit on my lap facing me."

Her arms tremble as she shifts her upper body up. I lean back and spread my legs apart, forcing her to take a wider stance as she straddles me. I scoot her hips forward so she's sitting right on the crotch of my jeans. I place my hand between her breasts. "Your heart is racing."

She bites down on her lip, no doubt feeling my cock twitch through the rough denim. "Did watching me struggle turn you on?"

I slide my hand down to her mound, stopping just shy of her clit. "We are animals, Roxy. Carnal fucking animals. We're designed to hunt, to trap, and to feed. But you are only at my mercy because you want to be. You could've gotten up at any time. I wouldn't have stopped you."

Her eyelids flutter, her nipples stiffening as I twirl my fingers through her thick tuft of pubic hair. She arches her back as the red flush across her skin deepens. "I need to cum. Please, Punk."

Mmm. I know she does. So fucking bad. But I'm not done breaking her. I spoon some of the melted ice cream up and hold it over the bowl between us. "After I'm done with my ice cream, then you can cum."

"You've got to be joking," she growls.

I dangle the spoon between us, taunting her. "I'm dead fucking serious."

"Let me help you, then." She huffs and frantically reaches for the spoon.

I dodge her attempt. "You're getting worked up again, Roxy."

Her nostrils flare, but she lets me spoon a little into her mouth. "That's it. Rub your pussy against me *nice and slow* while I enjoy my tasty treat."

A moan flutters out of her as she rolls her hips and slides back and forth. My cock is so hard, I try to focus on the sugary sweet vanilla cream in my mouth, willing myself not to burst.

She white-knuckles the armrests, stilling herself. "Fuck... I-I can't. I'm gonna cum."

My grin widens. I spoon three more bites into my mouth, giving her a brief respite until my patience starts to wane. I slap the back of the spoon against her swollen nipple. "I didn't say you could stop, pretty girl. Grind that pussy till it's raw."

"Punk, this is torture." She pants as she resumes. My jeans are soaked in her juices. The scent of her arousal is transcendent. I want to bury my face inside her. Fuck. I'm torturing myself.

I blow out a chuckle. "You'll thank me after."

Her eyes turn to half-slits as she moans deep and low. I scrape the bowl with my spoon, drawing it out just a little longer. Her body drips with sweat, glistening like she has a fever. The way she grinds her hips, arching her back as she hums to herself... she's the best fucking drug I've ever taken.

She sounds like a cat in heat, her moans and whimpers turning into whines. In her trance, she doesn't notice me set the bowl down. All that matters to her right now is obeying me. Pleasing me.

I reach underneath her to undo the button and zipper on my jeans. "Such a good fucking girl. Cum for me now. *Cum*, Roxy."

She lets out a wild screech as she bucks like a bull. I lift her hips up so I can free my cock. She lowers herself down onto it and keeps grinding. "Fuck. That's my pretty girl. Take your reward."

"Uhhh. Oh god. Mmm," she whines as she fists my hoodie. Her pussy is *soaking* wet. I can't hold back much longer.

I push her back so she's lying on my legs, half-upside down. "You're mine, Roxy." I dig my fingers into her fleshy hips and slam into her. "You fucking hear me?"

She braces her hands on the carpet to keep from banging her head. "Y-yes. Oh shit."

Her pussy feels like warm honey. Like a sacred vessel made only for my long, thick, veiny cock. Spasms start in my balls and spread in quick bursts down my shaft, charging my tip like electricity. I let out a grunt, pushing and pulling her to fit my length, stretching her as wide as her tender lips will allow.

"Punk," she whines as she claws at the carpet. "Cum inside me."

Mmm. Fuck. "You better hold on." I spring from the chair and stand with my cock deep inside her. I tuck my arms under her knees, my grip tight. She wraps her arms around my ankles while she's suspended upside down like a fucking acrobat. She might not dance anymore, but her muscles remember.

My stomach flutters as all the blood rushes from my balls to my swollen tip. I lower us both until her back is on the floor as I burrow in deeper, grinding in circles. "Roxy... *Fuck*," I grit out. My breath catches in my throat, and I almost black out as my cum floods her tight little pussy. I flick her clit, coaxing another orgasm out of her.

"Oh my god. Don't stop," she cries.

"I will rub you raw." I grind in circles, my cum still flowing. "Pray to me, pretty girl. Let me hear your hymns of devotion."

I keep punishing her clit with my thumb, rubbing it so hard she bites her bottom lip and draws blood. "Punk..."

I pull her up, bringing her with me as I sit back down in the chair. My cock pulses inside her as she trembles around it. "Let me hear how you worship me," I whisper in her ear.

She whimpers and wraps her arms around my neck. "*You're my god, Punk. I submit.*"

I tilt her chin up. "I will take care of you from now on, pretty little girl."

She gasps as I press my mouth to hers. Her lips are so soft and thick. I thrust my tongue inside and find hers just as demanding. Ravenous. She tastes like sweat and sex and wine. The closest I will ever get to heaven. We devour each other, hungrily exploring each other's mouths as we bite and suck, exchanging breath and saliva like sacrifices on a holy altar.

We stay like this for hours, kissing and caressing each other with my cock still inside her cunt. Like we are surgically attached. *I wish we were.* I'd stitch us together if I could. I never want to leave her holy cocoon.

When her head starts to droop on my shoulder, I reluctantly lift her off and tuck her into bed. I nestle up behind her, wrapping one arm around her waist and the other around her neck.

She coos softly while drifting off to sleep. "Don't leave, Jack... I mean Punk," she pleads quietly.

I kiss her on the cheek. "I'm not going anywhere. I'm never letting you go, Jilly girl. Never. Fucking. Ever."

My angel slept so hard she didn't wake once when I transferred her to my penthouse. Not while I carried her down the stairs. Not during the car ride—I left my bike behind and drove her car instead. My momma always said that it's better to ask for forgiveness rather than permission. This sensuous creature purred like a cat even as I held her in the elevator going up to my floor. She looks so peaceful in my bed. I'll savor it now. Because when she wakes up and sees I've tied her to the frame, I'm going to have a hell-hound on my hands.

Maybe that's what pushed Lucifer to finally fall.

It's for her own good. I want her to acclimate to her new surroundings first. I can't risk her storming off and doing something stupid. I don't mind killing for her. I rather enjoy it. But I want my pretty girl subdued for now. The longer she's contained, the wilder the beast when I finally unleash her. And then we will both cum so hard it'll be transcendent. Like two aliens discovering dark matter for the first time.

With Roxy still sleeping soundly, I oversee the movers. They've been packing up her apartment all morning and are finally carrying everything in. I lead them to the east wing of my penthouse and show them the various rooms I want her things set up in. Another bold move, but I just know that my pretty girl will love it here. I have her all to myself now.

I also took the liberty of texting Juniper from Roxy's phone.

Hey girl, I'm not feeling so great after last night. Can you work for me today?

Of course, Juniper replies back with a yes, along with a multitude of lewd and suggestive texts about me. I smirk as I read my favorite one.

Girrrl. You would've felt a lot better if you'd rode Punk Wilder's thick cock instead. At least your pussy would have. He's so into you!

Mmm. She has no idea how into Roxy I was last night. I chuckle to myself as I walk back into the bedroom to check on her.

Fucking hell, she is gorgeous. I amble forward and take a seat on the bed. The sight of her pink pussy partially covered by a luscious mound of dark pubic hair makes my glands salivate. I want a taste.

I skate the tips of my fingers up her thighs. She whimpers softly in response, her eyelids fluttering. I climb onto my king-size bed and nestle in between her legs. I suck on my finger before dragging it down her slit.

I shudder as my cock springs to life. She's so slick, even when she's asleep. Just primed and ready for me at all times. I peel the lips of her pussy back and gently stroke the inside of them. "This is mine now," I whisper.

I blow out a shaky breath and slowly insert my finger inside her hole, pushing through her soft folds. "Fuck. You're so tight."

She jerks her head to the side and moans.

"Yeah, I know what my pretty girl likes," I rasp as I insert a second finger. I curl them up and down, flicking her most sensitive spot as I massage her clit with my thumb.

She writhes and pants, her eyelids flutter open to half-slits. "Punk… what are you…"

"Shhh, relax. Submit to it." With my free hand, I retrieve a new anal plug from my jacket pocket. "This one is a size up, but I think you're really going to love the stretch."

I stick it in my mouth and suck on it, coating it with a thick layer of my saliva. I push her legs up and wedge the tip of it inside her ass.

Her eyes fly open, her gaze darting back and forth between me and her bound wrists. "Punk!" Her chest heaves as she struggles against the restraints. "What the fuck have you done? Where am I?"

I thrust my fingers in and out of her pussy. It makes her shudder, and her eyes roll back. "You're in my house. *Our house*. I'll give you a full tour once you calm down."

"What do you mean *our* house, Punk?" she says through another whimper.

I press against her G-spot, sending goosebumps over her flesh. "You live here with me now. The movers just finished bringing in all of your stuff. And don't worry about your old place. I paid your landlord what was left in your lease."

She gasps and looks around again. The decor in my bedroom is dark, masculine, and cold. But I know she'll bring a warmer touch to it.

She breathes deep as I play with her clit. "Fuck… mmm. Wait. You can't just move me without asking. That's not okay."

I shrug and thrust a third finger inside her soaking-wet pussy. "I want you here with me, safe. And I want you full of my cum every night. My place is bigger than yours. You will never want for anything. We can worship each other, pretty girl."

She lets out another moan as I pump faster. "We should've talked about this. I barely know you."

I give her pussy a light slap, eliciting a deeper moan. "You know me better than you think. And I know you better than anyone." I slap her pussy again, and she bucks. "I know what you like. What you want. What you love." I lean down and roll my tongue over her clit. "Don't you want this every night, Roxy?"

"Fuck… that feels so good… Mmm." She rolls her hips as she chases her orgasm.

"Thatta girl. Relax for me. Let me put this in." I press the tip of the plug to her mouth. "Get this nice and wet for me."

She moans and takes it in her mouth, soaking it with her saliva.

"Yeah, the wetter it is, the easier it will glide inside. Good girl."

I inch the tip in first and let her get used to the bigger fit for a second. Her juices leak down my wrists as I continue to thrust my fingers deep inside her cunt. Fuck, I could play with her like this all day and night. We might starve to death if I'm not careful.

"Fuck, it's thick, Punk," she whines.

"I know. But my cock is three times this, so we're going to break you in slow. Take a deep breath and open up for me." I push the glass plug in another inch, getting past the second bead. Each one is larger than the last. "You're doing so good. One more bead to go."

Roxy jerks her hips up. "It's too much. There's no fucking way it's gonna fit."

I grin down at her before releasing a wad of spit down her slit. She shudders as I smear it all the way back to her ass. "It will. I promise. And then it's going to feel so fucking good. Just think how hard you're going to cum when we start playing with it."

She bites down on her lip. "Fuck. Okay, fine. Just do it."

I reach over her to the bedside table and pull a tube of lube out of the drawer. "I'm going to make it hurt less. Saliva alone isn't cutting it."

I squirt a glob of it into my palm and reach underneath her. She raises her hips to allow me better access. "There we go. You feel that? It's already loosening up."

She nods. "Please, Punk. Just do it."

I chuckle and slide the rest of the plug inside. Her mouth gapes, forming an *O*, as the third and largest bead stretches her delicate hole to a size it's never been before. I give it a little twist to make sure it's fully snug.

"Ohhh, fuck." She pants, her chest heaving.

"This one doesn't vibrate, love. But we can still have some fun with it."

"Are you a psycho, Punk?" She gazes up at me with lust-glazed eyes.

I roll my thumb in circles around her clit. "We both are, Roxy. That's why we fit. No one else can make you feel this way. The way I touch you and fuck you. No one else. I'll kill anyone who tries. Tell me you feel the same way. Tell me you wouldn't murder a woman for touching me."

Her nostrils flare and her eyes narrow. She never thought about it before. But now she is. "No one better fucking touch you, Punk. I swear to fucking—"

I thrust hard, cutting her off with her own orgasm exploding in her core. "No one, baby. I'm yours. Now cum for your god. Cum all over my holy fucking hand."

CHAPTER 12

ROXY

THE WORD ORGASM DOESN'T JUSTIFY THE EXPLOSION IN MY CORE. There is nothing that can fully make sense of the sensations ripping through my body. In this moment, I'm locked in with him, sinking deeper and deeper into his transcendence.

I should be angry with him for uprooting my entire life. For stalking me, haunting my dreams, then tying me up and touching me while I slept. In theory, he's kidnapped me. Violated me. But is it wrong if I don't want him to stop?

Punk glides his wet fingers up and over my belly. He draws circles around my nipples, causing them to harden and ache. With a smirk on his face, he rakes them over my chest, my neck, and then pushes them into my mouth, forcing me to taste my own arousal. A deep moan billows out of me as I suck the salt and cum off his skin.

As he presses down on my tongue, he thrusts two new fingers

inside my pussy. I arch back and spread my legs as far as I can, allowing him to get deeper.

"We're insatiable together," he declares.

The stretch in my ass deepens the pressure in my core. I can feel him in my lower back, my belly, my fucking throat. His fingers slide back, and I convulse, gagging around them. But I'm distracted by the way he pushes against my G-spot. I forget to breathe for a second and almost black out.

"I will take you to hell and back, pretty girl. Hell is so much sweeter. Fuck, you feel so good when you surrender." He palms my pussy and squeezes it.

A feral sound escapes my throat, so monstrous I startle myself. I bite down on his fingers, drawing blood, as I roll my hips and grind against him. We lock eyes as I cum all over his hand.

My heart skips. *He's fucking gorgeous.* Photos don't do him justice. Neither did the lighting at Push that night we *bumped* into each other. Dirty-blond hair with waves I want to run my fingers through and eyes the lightest shade of hazel I've ever seen. Not to mention a jawline I want to suck on and thick lips that turn my nipples into live wires. This man *looks* like a god.

"I will wake you up like this every morning." He slowly draws his fingers away and sits back on his heels. He tilts his head to the side, studying my face. "If I untie you, do you promise to stay with me?"

I lick my lips, my throat dry. "Yes… but only if you promise to let me come and go as I please."

His devilish smirk returns. "Of course, you can, Roxy. You're not a prisoner. Besides, I will always be watching you. I can't risk anything happening to my pretty girl."

My belly does a little flip. Why the fuck does the idea of getting stalked by my own boyfriend turn me on? Fuck. Punk Wilder is my boyfriend now. "Good because I have a job that I semi-like and friends who I love hanging out with."

He leans over and unties my left wrist, chuckling to himself. "Well, just so you know, those two idiots you work with are the ones who told me your name and gamertag. I might have to have a little chat with them about that."

My stomach drops. "What the fuck? I'm going to murder them myself."

Punk wraps a hand around my throat and hovers over me. "Shhh, relax. Don't get worked up. We'll spare them since they helped bring us together."

I take short breaths as his grip tightens. A spasm flutters deep inside. Oh fuck. That's unexpected. "Okay," I rasp. Part of me wants to fight back so I can cum again. But I'm starving and need to pee. Not sure which order I want to do those in yet.

He frees my other wrist but stays straddling me. Something feral flashes in his eyes. "Those who exist outside these walls are nothing but pathetic sheep. They don't deserve to be in your presence. I tolerate it because it's what you want. But if anyone crosses a line, I will skin them alive. Remember that every time you leave this penthouse."

It's a warning, not a threat. Every person I come into contact with is in danger at all times. I shudder as I stare back at him. My juices trickle from my entrance, wetting my thighs. This is a brutal kind of love. One that has already started to consume me. His possessiveness makes me feel powerful, not weak. The tighter his grip, the harder I fall. The more I want to prove to him that I'm worthy of his obsession.

With my hands free, I slide them under his shirt and finger the ridges of his perfectly chiseled abs. "The world is at our mercy."

He grins and presses his soft lips against mine, a sweet kiss from a violent man who can shatter me just by looking at me. I lean into his embrace, wrapping my arms around his neck as our tongues find each other. It's a chaotic swirl of emotions that plays out in our fiery mouths.

I moan as our kiss deepens, clawing my fingers through his hair, desperate to swallow every drop of his saliva. I want his essence inside me. I wish I could crawl inside him and rest inside his bones. To feel his skin as my skin.

The grumble of my belly makes him pause. He chuckles. "I need to feed you. Come. Let me show you where I've put your things. I'll make you breakfast while you're getting dressed."

It takes me a few minutes to stabilize myself as I get up from the bed. His devotion has made me dizzy and lightheaded. I'm running on a high of lust and adrenaline. But I need actual sustenance so I don't pass out.

I gasp when we enter the living room. It's massive, with floor-to-ceiling windows. I press my naked body against the glass and look down. "You can see the whole city from here."

He nestles up behind me, his cock pulsing against my lower back. "Roxy, if you don't get dressed right now, you're going to starve to death. Because I will fuck you against this window for the next three hours."

Oh fuck. I don't know how we're ever going to keep our hands off each other. I let out a little sigh. "Starving doesn't sound so bad when you put it like that." I slither out of his embrace. "But you're right. Show me the rest."

He leads me into another primary bedroom except there isn't a bed. The center of the room is occupied by multiple stacks of boxes. To the left is a door that leads into an ensuite bathroom. And next to that is another door that opens up to a closet the size of my old apartment. All my clothes are hung up neatly and arranged by color.

He leans against the doorframe. "I had the movers hang up your clothes to my liking, but I figured you didn't want them rifling through your things again. You can put them anywhere you want in our house."

Our house. That was going to take some getting used to. Other than my piece-of-shit stepfather, I've never lived with a man before. "Thank you, Punk. I'll just wash up a little and meet you in the kitchen?"

He stalks behind me again and squeezes my ass. "Yes, it's just off the living room." He slips his fingers inside my anus and curls them around the plug. "We can play with this again later, pretty girl."

I grab onto the closet's doorframe to brace myself. Tingles spread through my core as he pulls on it. It's a mixture of relief and ache. I clench around the last bead, not quite ready to lose the sensation.

He caresses my belly with his free hand as he twists the tip of the plug in circles a few times. "I got you a whole set of these, pretty girl," he croons in my ear. "All different sizes and shapes." He teases my entrance with it, pushing and pulling back and forth.

I whimper and press my forehead against the frame. Sweat beads on my temples. "Can you give me another one after breakfast? Please, Punk…"

His breath is hot on my face. "Yes, baby… but only if you let me feed you."

I nod furiously. I'll promise him anything. *I'll give him anything*. Just to always feel like this.

He twists the plug one more time before pulling it out. He sweeps my hair to the side and nuzzles my neck. "You're doing so good. The more you submit, the greater the rewards."

A shiver dances across my back. There is no going back now. I belong to this man. Body, mind, and soul—I'm his.

Punk prepares our plates at the center island, shirtless and barefoot. His hair is damp, and he smells of powdery soap and fresh linen. He grins over at me when I walk in, freshly showered as well. Dressed in black yoga pants and a thin white tank top, I wonder how long before he strips me out of them. I love being naked with him. I crave it.

"After the first time I followed you, after catching your scent, I stocked all the bathrooms with peach soaps and body washes. I even had a bowl of peaches in here. And every time I ate one, I'd imagine it was your sweet cunt. I'm going to eat it off you next time. Can you imagine? All those juices dripping together… Mmm."

My face flushes, spreading a feverish heat across my skin. I'm suddenly shy, nervous by the way he looks at me. The way he speaks. "I… yes." How does one respond to that? Like yes, please. Right fucking now. You can absolutely use that insanely hot tongue of yours to lick peach juice out of my pussy. Good lord.

He winks and motions to the barstool. "Sit. Food's ready." He carries a bowl of fresh fruit, yogurt, and granola to me, holding a spoonful of it between us. "No more junk food except on cheat days. Now open up, pretty girl."

I smile and take the creamy bite into my mouth. He's making

me better and healthier. "You're so good to me. I knew you would be."

He caresses my throat. "I love watching you swallow."

"I love watching *you*," I murmur.

He drags my stool closer to his and leans forward. "I know, pretty girl… I know *everything*." He drags his thumb across my lower lip, tugging it down. "I followed your breadcrumbs. Every tasty little morsel you left for me to find…"

My breath quickens. Fuck. The blood in my head rushes to my feet. "What are you—"

His grip around my throat tightens, restricting my airflow. "Shhh. I saw you, Roxy. The day of my accident. You were there in the crowd… How could I forget your pretty face?" He licks the side of my cheek, slowly dragging his tongue from my jaw up to my temple. "*You* made sure Vinyl Delights sponsored the party at Joystick because you were hoping I'd show up. Am I right?"

Fuck. Stars dot my vision as his fingers dig into the sides of my neck. *He knows*. I claw at his hand, but it's no use. I'm at his mercy. Tears stream down my cheeks.

He laps them up with his sinful tongue. "Shhh, it's okay, baby. Your obsession brought me back to life. And now you're mine to do whatever I want with."

"When did you know?" I rasp.

"Oh, my lovely little fangirl… I knew the second I saw you. And then when those idiots revealed everything about you… You inspired my gamertag. *The Jack to your Jill*. Isn't it clever?" He releases my throat only to grab the back of my head and yank me forward till I'm standing between his legs. He smirks as he gazes down at me. "I knew I had to keep you. No one loves me the way you do, pretty girl. And now nothing will ever come between us."

Fuck. I never thought in a million years that he'd actually notice me. I ball my fists to keep my fingers from trembling. He set the trap and I walked right into it. "I've had a crush on you for so long. I should've told you that last night… You're not angry?"

He frees his cock from his sweatpants and rolls his thumb over the tip, coaxing his pre cum out. "How could I be angry with my Jilly girl? The way you worship me at my altar, my obedient little disciple. Mmm, you've got me so obsessed. But if you ever try to leave me, I'll kill you."

My belly flutters as my juices soak my panties. "Never. I promise, Punk. I won't leave you."

He fingers my lips. "Shhh, on your knees."

I lower myself to the floor in between his legs. "Punish me."

His eyes light up and that devilish smirk returns. "Oh, I plan to. Open your mouth and relax your throat. Yeah, just like that. My naughty little slut."

I flinch as he thrusts his thick veiny cock all the way in, hitting the back of my throat with violent force. I gasp for breath as he holds my head and slowly fucks my mouth. I roll my tongue over every ridge, moaning through the tears that spill down my cheeks.

"This isn't just a *crush*, Roxy. It's a holy fucking sacrament. And you will drink every drop of my cum as your penance." *Thrust.* "Oh, baby. Fuck." *Thrust.* "We're gonna do really bad fucking things together."

He punishes my mouth, bruising my lips and the insides of my cheeks. My teeth rake against his shaft, which only makes him moan louder. Over and over, each thrust hits harder than the last as he claims me. I suck and lick, feral for the taste of him.

I gag as his cum bursts in my mouth. My throat convulses as I try to swallow and fight for air at the same time. I dig my nails into his thighs and take slow deep breaths through my nose.

"Thatta girl. Fuck. Drink the nectar from your god." He wraps his hand around my throat so he can feel it bob in his hand.

I don't stop until I've sucked him clean. Breathless and dizzy, I lean against him. "I love the way you taste."

He tilts my chin up to look into my eyes. "I love *you*, pretty girl."

A warm tingling spreads like wildfire in my belly. "I love you too." He's mine. *Punk Wilder is finally mine.*

EPILOGUE

ROXY

THE BROKEN PORCH LIGHT FLAPS IN THE WIND. HANGING BY A single wire, it flickers, illuminating the chipped, green paint on the siding of my momma's single-wide trailer. A shiver snakes up my back. All the lights are off inside. But I know he's here.

"You sure you want to do this? I can go in and take care of it." Punk stands next to me in the dirt, dressed in all black, his face concealed beneath a glow-in-the-dark mask.

I nod but keep my eyes trained on the front door. "I need to finish what I started. He took so much from me…"

"It's quiet out here, Roxy. There's no one around for miles. We can take our time. But you still need to put this on. Just in case."

A rush of adrenaline courses through my veins when he

hands me my doll mask. I put it on without hesitating. It feels like armor. I become the mask. The broken doll who's had enough.

"*Good girl,*" he whispers in my ear. "Now we can play."

Every night, my momma heads into town for her overnight shift at the motel. And my step-father spends that time drinking himself into a blacked-out stupor. When I was a kid, I'd hide in the woods until I saw the headlights of her rusty pickup truck round the final bend of the dirt trail.

I clench my fists as I remember him flying out of the trailer when he'd hear the clank of the truck door slamming shut. I'd creep closer, hiding in the bushes, scared and angry that I was too small to help her. He'd slap her around and then take whatever tips she'd earned that night.

As I got older, my anger turned toward her. Because she wouldn't help *herself.* And when I got tits and curves, his attention turned toward me...

"It will all be over soon, pretty girl. He will pay his penance owed to you." Punk wraps my hand around the hilt of his serrated hunting knife. "Make him squeal like the pig he is."

That same terracotta planter still sits on the porch, dead flowers and weeds drooping over its sides. I kick it over to find the spare key right where I left it. I hold my breath as I turn it in the lock. The door creaks open on its rusted hinges, but the monster inside is too drunk to notice.

Punk heads in first, using his body as a protective shield. I draw in a sharp breath as that familiar scent finds its way to my nostrils—cheap beer, cigarette smoke, and dirty laundry. I almost vomit inside my mask.

I creep around Punk to get a closer look at the remnants of

my childhood. The prison that I traded for another when I failed to put him down. I won't make that mistake twice.

He's in his favorite spot, an old brown office chair that he stole from a yard sale. His sweaty pot belly hangs over the waist of his boxers. I inch forward, possessed, thirsty for blood. The light from the moon streaks over him, highlighting the scowl that never leaves his face. Not even when he sleeps.

I take my time zip-tying his ankles. Then I do the same to his wrists, binding them to the arms of the chair he loves so much. The one he's about to die in.

"Careful," Punk whispers.

I nod and press the tip of the blade to his neck. "Wake up, asshole."

Punk slaps him across the face.

His eyes fly open, widening when he sees the doll-faced figure staring back at him. "What the fuck?"

"Did you miss me, Hank?"

"Roxanne? You stupid bitch." As he jerks forward, Punk grabs his shoulders and pulls him back against the chair.

"Shhh. No one can hear you. Remember?" I drag the tip of the blade across his heaving chest. "Isn't that what you used to tell me when I cried?"

His gaze shifts to Punk. "This bitch is crazy. You can't believe anything that comes out of her mouth."

Punk thrusts his thumb into Hank's right eye. "Call her a bitch one more time, and I'll fucking blind you."

Hank's gurgled cries exude the stale stench of liquor on his breath.

"Not yet, love. I want him to see what I do to him." My belly flips with excitement. I trace the blade over his cheek, lapping up some of the blood that drips from his eye. I relish the purple bruise that's starting to form under it.

"You're going straight to fucking jail again, Roxanne. But this time you ain't getting out. I'll make sure of it," he slurs.

I tilt my head to the side, wishing I could see myself through his eyes. "I think I'll start with your fingers first. They've been very naughty."

A rush of adrenaline surges through me when I slice into his index finger. Punk covers Hank's mouth as he screams. I take my time sawing through the bone. "There. Only nine more to go."

Hank's face pales, and he slumps back in his chair. "I'm sorry. Please stop. I promise I'll never touch you again."

I snicker and repeat the process to his middle finger. "It's too late for that." His screams are deafening as I chop off his ring finger. "I didn't come here for apologies. I came for blood. For vengeance. *For penance.*"

I don't stop until his hand is nothing but a bloody stump. I am not Roxanne Luna anymore. I'm not even Roxy right now. I'm Punk's disciple. I'm JillChick22. I'm the doll he ripped apart at the seams. But each pound of flesh I take, stitches another piece of me back together.

"He'll black out before you finish his other hand. Time to end this, pretty girl," Punk commands.

I nod in submission. But not out of weakness or lack of control. But because Punk is the only man I'll ever submit to. I'm his sacred vessel. The light that his darkness is safe to roam in. Both our broken pieces fit together like a mosaic that's been hidden for centuries. His fragments are mine, and mine are his.

I point the tip of the knife to his throat, pricking his skin. "Any last words, Hank?"

He glares up at me with his one good eye. "You'll never be anything else but daddy's little whore. You filthy fucking—"

Punk yanks my wrist forward, plunging the knife into Hank's throat. "That's about enough out of you." We do it together, slicing through until the tip of the blade exits the back of his neck.

My body goes rigid, my muscles stiff, as I watch the beast of my nightmares die in front of me. "And you'll always be dead," I whisper in his ear.

When his head slumps to the side, Punk helps me pull the knife out. It's not as easy as it looks on TV. There's so much tissue to cut through.

He takes the knife from me and sets it on the coffee table. Then he gathers me in his arms. "Jack is so proud of you, Jilly girl."

As my adrenaline plummets, I start to shake. "I-I did good, right?"

He takes off his mask and nudges me back against the coffee table, forcing me to sit down on it. "You were magnificent. My beautiful angel of death. You deserve a reward. Lay back."

A spasm flickers inside my cunt. Oh fuck. "You mean… here?"

He kneels between my legs and pushes my dress up to my waist. "Yes. In this place of death and rebirth." He slides my panties off and spreads my thighs. "Now, I'm going to baptize you with my tongue."

He peels my pussy lips back and licks me from taint to clit. Over and over again like a cat lapping at a bowl of milk. I thrust the bloody knife into the coffee table, using it as an anchor. I squeeze the hilt for dear life as Punk flicks against my clit then back down my slit again.

"Fuck," I cry out. "Why does that feel so good? Fuck."

"Shhh, let me sanctify you," he coos as he continues to stimulate every nerve in my pussy with just the flat of his tongue. He pinches my pussy lips back with his tattooed fingers. There is nothing gentle about this. Nothing sweet. It's raw and carnal.

My hips buck as my orgasm ignites deep inside my core and spreads like wildfire. I cum hard, screaming as I shatter and squirt all over his tongue. He laps ferociously at my cream, like a rabid animal who's been starved for days. I grind into his mouth, stretching out every agonizing spasm while the corpse of my monster lies bloody beside me.

My heart beats so fast I can barely breathe. Punk pulls me upright. "And from the ashes, she rises, glorious, transformed, and full of fire." He kisses the lips of my plastic doll mask.

I wrap my arms around his neck. Something has changed in me. Altered. It's a high unlike any other. "I would die a thousand deaths to feel this way again."

He grins back at me. "Let's play a new game then. Who else has hurt you, pretty girl?"

I push my mask up and gasp. He's giving me another gift. "My ex. After I destroyed my knee, I caught him fucking the girl who took my place on the dance team. He dumped me a few days after I lost my scholarship. He said I wasn't useful to him anymore."

Punk's eyes darken. A flicker of hunger, disease, and amusement contort his features. "Let's go. I can't wait to meet him."

I throw my arms around him again and sigh against his chest. "I don't know what I'd do without you."

He holds two fingers to my lips, and I obey without hesitation. I don't need words to know what he wants. When I open my mouth, he presses down on my tongue and slides his fingers to the back of my throat.

FETCH

"You will never be without me, pretty girl… Every Jack must have his Jill."

I gag on his fingers as we lock eyes. We are fated. Star-crossed lovers destined to find each other. Like Romeo and Juliet. Except instead of dying for love…

We kill for it.

MORE BOOKS BY M VIOLET

ACKNOWLEDGEMENTS

Thank you for reading FETCH! This novella is my ode to my love of gaming. When I'm not writing, I love to drink wine and play games on my Xbox so this was so fun for me to write! This was also my first MF stalker romance and I think I'm addicted to writing it now. There will definitely be more novellas to come in the gritty neon world of Lavender Heights.

I'd like to thank my amazing editor, Kat Wyeth, of Kat's Literary Services. You have been with me since Good Girl and I'm so grateful to have you on my team!

Thank you to my PA, Darcy Bennett! As always, your friendship and support means everything to me. Thank you for being the best PA an author could ever ask for!

Thank you to Coffin Print Designs for this stunning cover! It turned out exactly as I pictured it! And I've been having a blast making graphics to go with it.

Thank you to Stacey of Champagne Book Design for formatting FETCH! I cannot express enough how grateful I am to have you on my team!

Thank you to my VIXENS!!! Whether you're on my Street Team, ARC Team, or hang out in the group to support me and my books, I am so lucky and happy and grateful and blessed to have you all on this journey with me. Thank you STREET TEAM for your support, your enthusiasm, and your loyalty. It means so much. Thank you ARC TEAM for your excitement to read every book I release. Thank all of you for just being a really awesome group of humans. I love you so much!

Thank you to all my BADASS AND BEAUTIFUL friends! A.L. Maruga, Cassie Fairbanks, Candi Scott, Renee, The Smutven, and Write Club! I'm obsessed with all of you and I love you so much.

And last but never least, Thank you to my family for all your support. I would not be able to do this without you. Especially Mama Vixen, Dad, my sister Jen, and Mr. Violet. Thank you for never judging me for what I write. I am so blessed to have you in my pod.

Until next time, lovelies.

M Violet
XOXO

ABOUT THE AUTHOR

M Violet is a dark romance author with a flair for the dramatic. She likes whiskey, rainy nights, and writing by the fire. When she's not creating scorching hot villains for you to fall in love with, you can find her eating chocolate and binge watching her favorite shows.

Facebook: Authormviolet
Instagram: Authormviolet
Tik Tok: Authormviolet
Website: mvioletbooks.com

www.ingramcontent.com/pod-product-compliance
Lightning Source LLC
Chambersburg PA
CBHW061523050726
47503CB00015B/2687